PRAISE FOR REVENGE IN 3 PARTS

"...a striking and complicated protagonist."
"...genuinely surprising plot turns."
*"...a whirlwind of deceit, theft, blackmail,
and worse."*
—Kirkus Review

"Beware of disguises and those who wear them. Val Brooks has crafted a cunning tale of revenge, grief and unwanted desire that lets you walk the streets of Paris, Portland, and Kauai as bereft sister, confident attorney, vengeful murderer, and confused lover. By the time you're done, you and your anxious narrator are left wondering which of those identities you'll need to go on living with yourself."
—Paul Skenazy, former thriller reviewer *Washington Post*, and author of *James M. Cain*

"*Revenge in Three Parts* is a swift, seductive, menacing

tale of extortion and murder. Like the great James M. Cain, Brooks strips her story down to the bare essentials, effortlessly blending classic noir (urban settings, unexpected narrative detours, a suspicious money trail) with uniquely modern components, including a professional computer hacker, Snapchat, and the Ashley Madison dating site. With its breakneck pace, intriguing cast of characters, and unabashed eroticism, *Revenge in Three Parts* is a wild, wicked, and utterly delightful ride."

--Tim Applegate, *Fever Tree*

"The author treats you to a strong intelligent, gutsy woman who writes her own rules and throws herself into a dangerous situation of her own creation. As has been said, 'well-behaved women seldom make history'—or good novels."

—Wendy Kendall, "Kendall and Cooper Talk Mysteries" podcast

"Revenge is a dish best served hot, at least in Valerie Brooks' *Revenge in Three Parts,* a sexy fast-paced tale of family, love, and murder. Brooks' settings are characters too: two-faced lovers who charm as they kill. Can't wait for Brooks' next noir!"

—Cindy Brown, Agatha-nominated author of the Ivy Meadows mystery series

"Jan Myrdal famously said, 'Traveling is like falling in love; the world is made new.' In *Revenge in Three Parts*, Valerie J. Brooks offers up a darker, if no less enthralling view of globetrotting. With *Revenge*, we follow jaded criminal lawyer Angela Porter as she seeks to avenge her sister's tragic death. With a whip-crack voice and delicious twists, *Revenge* is a thoroughly engrossing page-turner."

—Bill Cameron, author of the award-winning Skin Kadash mysteries

"Button up your trench coat! Valerie J Brooks' *Revenge in Three Parts* puts an original twist on the classic elements of noir. *Revenge* successfully and poignantly balances travel destinations with the darkest compulsions of the human heart. Brooks' future travel destinations promise more creatively chilling mysteries!"

—Chris Scofield, author of *The Shark Curtain*

"*Revenge in Three Parts* in twist after twist keeps our senses reeling as Angeline, an ex-attorney who believes in ultimate justice, comes closer and closer to the truth of why her sister committed suicide. Follow Angeline to the edge. Does she ever find what she seeks? Is she willing to go for the ultimate revenge, one that might tear her own life apart or even take her life? Find out in this tense noir mystery set in Paris, Portland, Oregon, and Kauai."

--Patsy Hand, *Lost Dogs of Rome*

REVENGE IN 3 PARTS

VALERIE J. BROOKS

BLACK LEATHER JACKET PRESS

ISBN 978-1-7323732-0-4 (paperback)
ISBN 978-1-7323732-1-1 (e-book)
Library of Congress Control Number: 2018907933

For Daniel

"There are crimes of passion and crimes of logic. The boundary between them is not clearly defined."

—Albert Camus

"The dead cannot cry out for justice. It is the duty of the living to do so for them."

—Lois McMaster Bujold

PART I

1

As I walked down Boulevard de Grenelle, I was tired, cranky, and not used to having men stare at me. The blonde wig I wore over my usual brunette bob made my scalp sweat and itch. And where was the seasonal weather? Around noon, three days before Christmas, and I wore sunglasses, a lightweight coat, scarf, and a silk shift? I never wore dresses. Paris in winter, and it's sunny and mild?

Better than freezing rain, I told myself.

But freezing rain would have better fit my mood.

My arm ached from hauling my carry-on behind me and slinging it on and off the train, then up and down the Metro stairs. I didn't care. The Metro was my ally, reminding me of why I'd come to Paris. A large photo of Marilyn Monroe hung above Metro entrances and exits, an advertisement for a Halsman photography exhibit at Jeu de Paume. Monroe sat cross-legged and gorgeous on the floor, barefoot, naked shoulders, bra strap hanging, head bent over a book. So much like my sister Sophie, so vulnerable, so precious, you wanted to wrap a blanket around her and say come with me, anything to keep her from ever being hurt again.

But I didn't wrap that blanket around Sophie, and now my sister was dead.

Another Metro line clattered overhead. I shivered as my energy waned and my spirits sank into the gray of the neighborhood, the lack of holiday lights, the doubts of whether or not I could pull this off. The 15th arrondissement was unfamiliar to me. Years before, when my husband Hank and I stayed in Paris, we rented apartments in the Marais, a more upscale area. This area was a working-class neighborhood even though it's only a ten-minute walk to the Eiffel Tower. I probably wouldn't have chosen this arrondissement—if I'd had a choice.

But the Frenchman lived here, and he'd killed my sister.

He'd also killed my unborn niece or nephew.

A man stopped to appraise me. I shoved past him and walked by three souvenir shops. From one shop the song "Hotel California" played on a cheap boombox. I hated that song. As I approached a neighborhood supermarket, the Franprix, a beggar dressed in the saddest Santa outfit I'd ever seen sat on the sidewalk and held out his paper cup. He looked up at me. I shivered, glanced away, and hurried past.

The apartment was somewhere nearby. I couldn't wait to take off the wig and all the make-up—foundation, blush, eye-shadow, eyeliner, mascara, the works. I never wore this crap and felt as phony as that Santa suit. When you worked at a law firm like mine, conservative dress was a given. I preferred to call it classic. But I wasn't in Paris as me, Angeline Porter. I was here as journalist Helen Craig.

I searched for the address of my apartment. Square Desaix, Square Desaix, where the hell was Square Desaix? I found the street. A flower shop decorated for the season sat on the corner. That brightened my mood somewhat. I turned up the dead-end road to the address and rang the bell. The "guardian," a concierge of sorts, greeted me and gave me the key. I remembered little French, but I managed. When I tried to cram into the phone-booth-size elevator with my carryon, I couldn't, so I put my suitcase on the lift, pressed button three, and walked up the curved staircase to the third floor. I grabbed my suitcase, unlocked the apartment door, and stepped into the three-room rental, spacious by Paris standards. In the bedroom, I pulled off my wig and boots, collapsed on the bed, and fell asleep.

Two hours later I woke with a start. It was late afternoon. Back home it was the middle of the night. I made coffee with the stash in the cupboard, pulled back the curtains on the French doors, stepped onto the wrought iron balcony with its potted red geraniums, still blooming. Down on Grenelle, two women on the corner talked and smoked while their small dogs sniffed each other.

Parisians headed home after work, carrying bags of groceries, baguettes, briefcases. Cars tailgated, honked for no reason, played hip-hop music loud enough for me to hear. A flutter of homesickness hit, a wave of loss so strong I almost folded into a fetal, fucking mess. I didn't want Sophie to be dead. I dreaded knowing that my sister's personal effects, including the blue dress, would be waiting for me when I returned. I'd refused to let the funeral director cremate her in that abomination. Instead, she'd worn her favorite dusty rose dress with birds on it, the one she wore when we last went to the movies when I'd been too judgmental to recognize her pain.

On the dining room table, I spread out the papers from my file on the Frenchman. He lived off Rue du Commerce not far from here. On my burner phone, I Google-mapped the address.

"You're dead, Gerard Duvernet. Hear me? Dead."

I kept my revenge well-fueled. All I had to do was picture Sophie's body hanging from the hook in her living room, wearing that blue dress he'd bought her.

2

A week before Sophie died, we were watching Daniel Craig in "Spectre" at her place. She was quiet, unusually so.

Sophie worked from home, a brilliant nerd in a beautiful body. Because she looked like Marilyn Monroe, people underestimated her. I called her an IT person which she flatly denied, but she knew all about code, and God knew what else. So I said, "You're an 'it girl' then." She laughed. In her spare time, she had designed online games for women while fighting the abusive male-dominated game establishment. She was discerning, passionate and brave in her gaming world, but not in the real world.

Sophie was generous with her love, but not discerning. Hank said she made terrible choices and focused too much on the details—the way the man moved, the number of texts he sent in a day, the way the man noticed what she did with her hair, the books the guy read, the movies he picked, whether he ate meat or not. Hank said she missed the big picture—the guy had failed in three businesses; the guy was a control freak; the guy paid alimony and child support to two ex-wives; the guy had never been in a long-term relationship.

Usually, Sophie told me about the latest guy in detail and asked my opinion. I said what I thought. I made suggestions. If the guy seemed questionable, I offered to check his record.

"Oh, Ang," she said. "You're too cynical."

"Damn right. If you worked in the criminal justice system, you would be too."

That night she remained silent.

Finally, I asked, "Who is he? And what's up?"

Sophie pulled a photo from her purse. In the photo, Sophie and man stood in front of a classy sign for the Miami Business Fair, an exhibit of professionals trying to attract investors. One of Sophie's clients had created a collagen product that promised to replace Botox and, knowing the value of having a gorgeous woman to lure people to the booth, the client had paid Sophie a generous fee and all her expenses to model at their booth.

She said, "He's super sexy. He looks like Daniel Craig."

In the photo, Gerard Duvernet, tall, gracefully graying, good bone structure, a weak chin, smiled down at Sophie. He wasn't bad looking, but he was no Daniel Craig.

"I love him, Ang," she finally said. "I love him with all my heart. He's not like all the rest."

I'd heard similar sentiments before. "OK. Does this Daniel Craig love you?" She nodded. More tears. "Do you have a plan?"

She shook her head. "He's married with a son, and he's French, lives in France." She paused. "Don't you dare say anything. We're both heartbroken about this."

What could I say? I couldn't remember the last time a love affair had caused her this much pain. She had to be in love with him, but this was hopeless. France? A wife and kid? And he was probably Catholic.

"It's killing me," she said. "Gerard, too."

Yeah, I bet.

"Don't make a face, or roll your eyes." She glared at me. "He's going to leave her."

Fucking great. How cliché. How stupid. I noticed the Frenchman hadn't offered to get a divorce. I kept my mouth shut though. I needed to know more.

Sophie let out a long, noisy sigh and looked down at her lap. "It's complicated and messy, Ang. You have no idea what's going on." She snuffled back tears. "I hate myself. I truly do."

"Don't say that, Sophie." I squatted next to her chair and took her hands in mine. When she burst into tears, I said, "What can I do?"

She choked on a sob, her cheeks flushed red, and snot dripped from her nose. I handed her a tissue.

Sophie abruptly stood and shook her head. "I don't know what to do. I'm at the end of my rope," she said.

I held her. "Do the right thing, Sophie. Do what's right for you, not this Gerard character."

"But I love him." She choked out, "I'm so sorry."

I'd been through this with her many times. I knew her M.O. In the morning when she was calmer, she would call me. She always called after the emotional geyser. I figured she was sorry for always involving me in her love life. I *was* exhausted with her life with men. I held her even though I was thinking, *Who cares? They never last long.*

Now I cared. Big time.

Now my flippancy made me sick. I remembered Sophie's face, her downturned eyes, tears coursing down her cheeks.

She couldn't look at me. My sister. God, how I wished I hadn't been so unkind.

Sophie, my smart, generous sister, had always been kind. And now she was dead. Sophie would have been the best mom. She'd always wanted a child. She just couldn't recognize a decent man when she saw one.

3

The next morning, I called her and insisted on taking her to lunch. With Hank gone, I reminded her how much fun we'd have over the holidays. We weren't religious. We would shop at the Eugene Holiday Market craft fair, go to late night indie films at the Broadway Metro, eat Thai takeout from Sabai, and stream movies, as we always did when Hank was gone.

At Marché Restaurant, Sophie seemed jumpy. Even when she asked how Hank was and if I'd heard from him, she mixed her words and tripped over her tongue. I had to have her repeat what she said. She loved stories about Hank and his work, but I had nothing to tell her. I reminded her that he was out of satellite reach and so no communication. She picked at her lunch and mumbled things I couldn't hear. I noticed she wasn't wearing makeup. I'd never seen her outside her apartment without makeup.

Her demeanor reminded me of how she had been when she'd finally told me about her rape. We were young, still in school. She'd supposedly been safe at a girlfriend's sleep-over. My parents hadn't heard the phone ring when she'd called. I hadn't either. At the time, I was a good sleeper. The next day, when she came home, she wasn't the same. Sophie was nervous, jumpy, introverted. She stayed in her room. Beautiful as a movie star, Sophie had no dates for two years. Later she swore me to secrecy and told me what had happened. The girlfriend's father had raped her when she used the bathroom in the middle of the night. Now, it was too late for justice or retribution. The family had moved.

I'd been so angry, I yelled, "Why didn't you tell me?"

She shrunk back. "Her father threatened to kill me if I told anyone."

"As if!" I said. "Did you really think he'd kill you?"

"No, but I was afraid of what *you'd* do. I just wanted to forget."

"Me? What I'd do? Jeez, Sophie. I'd—"

"Ang, you would have done something to him, like put sugar in his gas tank, or break his windows, or tag his house. Or worse."

Evidently, she'd thought of payback and had some good ideas. My ideas came under the heading "or worse," complete with sneaky ways of not getting caught. I couldn't blame her for being scared. Reporting the father would have accomplished nothing except to haunt my sister's life.

Sitting across from her in the restaurant, I'd tried to forget the memory and sipped my scotch, ate my oysters. I'd had a bad week at work and Hank wasn't home to talk to, so I'd hoped to talk her. I patted the napkin to my mouth. "You do know that Hank is in the Chinese hinterlands, trying to find a place for his factory? He went there for the agricultural land. A perfect area to raise what he needs for his vegetable-based polyals."

She nodded. "Yes, I know. He told me." Then she finally asked about my job.

I was miffed. When I had something upsetting in my life, she always seemed to have a situation that kept me from telling her. I didn't want to add to her troubles. I'd always been the stronger one, the one that protected her, even when I was hurting. I hesitated, but ended up telling her about the head of the firm who had cornered me in his office, put his hand on my breast, and said I should be up for a partnership soon. I tried not to show how angry I was or what this could mean, but at that moment I wished I'd had a sister who would listen instead of being distracted. No, not distracted. Not even there. I was so pissed I said, "He was such a louse, I killed him."

"What?" she mumbled, trying to shake off the veil between us.

Under my breath, I said a sharp, "Hey! Snap out of it. Did you hear what I said?"

She looked down and let that curtain of striking blonde hair fall forward, hiding her heart-shaped face.

I reached for her hand. She pulled away. I grabbed my scotch and downed a slug. "Sophie, can't you see you're a mess? This man is not good for you."

"I don't want to talk about it, OK?"

I needed more than one scotch for this. My nerves were shot. With worrying about Sophie, I'd forgotten to take my anti-anxiety medication that morning. Without the meds, I couldn't work.

"Is it the Frenchman? I know you're booty-over-brains about him, but you seem too distraught for it to be just that."

"Forget it," she'd said. Then she drained her wine glass. "Leave me alone."

I swallowed the rest of my scotch and sat back. I was

worried about her while at the same time I was angry with her. For once, I would have liked some support.

I should have stayed with her that afternoon, insisted, but I went home in a huff instead. I figured she'd call like she usually did after she realized she'd been a shit.

But this time she didn't.

4

When she didn't call that night, I called her. But she didn't answer. In the morning, I called her from work, but her cell went to voicemail. I left a message and sent a text. I figured she had had a bad night, stayed up late, bingeing on television as she did sometimes when she was upset. She was probably sleeping.

By noon, I had what I can only describe as a choking feeling. I couldn't seem to get enough air. I left work and drove to Sophie's house. She didn't answer. My nerves were shredded, and I searched my purse three times before finding Sophie's extra apartment key. Then I struggled to get the key into the lock. When I opened the door, I knew I was too late.

From the hallway, I headed to the kitchen. In the living room, I found Sophie hanging there, profiled in the filtered light of her curtains. I didn't scream. I didn't understand people who screamed—at a rat, a spider, or a dead person.

My body turned icy. In my head, a message repeated: *that was not my sister, that was not my sister, that was not my sister.* I didn't look up at her face. I knew what hanging does to a face. Instead, I stared at her perfect feet with those perfect toes painted light coral. Sophie had never gone for bright colors. I had to call the police. Or was it the coroner? I touched Sophie's feet. Two of her toes clenched like fists. I pressed her feet together, those that had often rubbed against mine while we'd snuggled under a blanket watching a movie at her place, drinking cherry colas, eating buttery popcorn. Her feet were like little animals, seeking contact, warmth, and protection.

But I hadn't protected them—or her. I leaned in and pressed my face against her ankles, smelled the rose-scented body cream she used every night, and stifled a sob, thinking she'd done her usual nighttime regimen and for what? To kill herself?

I was about to lose it when I noticed the hem of her dress. I stepped back. The blue dress Gerard had brought from Paris. A gift to celebrate their four months together. It fit perfectly, from her broad, gorgeous shoulders to her small waist. It fell just above her knees. I'd never seen it on her. I turned away. A hot, sweaty flush broke over my body. I had to wipe my hands on my coat before shakily calling 911. Before the police arrived, I searched through her purse, found the photo of her and Gerard, and his business card. When I checked her phone and laptop, I discovered she had changed her passcode.

5

After the police, the inquiry, the memorial, the cremation, I carried an anger that threatened to crush me. Hank was not here to lift me out of my anger, but that was good because I didn't want him involved.

Hank couldn't leave China yet as he was working on a top-secret project for his chemical engineering firm, a place with no connectivity, not unusual. He knew nothing about the Frenchman. Sophie had sworn me to secrecy about the affair because Hank would have disapproved if he knew. Hank was like a big brother to her. She could disappoint me, but not him.

With Hank not knowing Sophie was dead, I was free to plan. He would never know what I was about to do, not this time.

Hank knew I'd flaunted the law before. The law firm where I'd worked had defended a rapist, an influential land developer running for state rep. Everyone had known he was guilty. Our firm got him off.

Four years later, the same guy, now a state rep, was

accused of rape again. Some of the evidence was damning, and our team suppressed it. I detested the sleaze-bag, the power he'd abused. So I secretly copied the evidence and slipped it to the prosecution. The rapist went to jail.

Distressed and fearing I was no better than the perpetrator in breaking the law, I told Hank. What if he found me reprehensible?

Thankfully, he poured me a whiskey and said, "He would rape other women, Ang. Maybe, eventually, kill someone. Could you live with that?"

I cried and shook my head. No, I couldn't.

But now I was older, and this was different. I couldn't share my plan with anyone.

I took two weeks off from work, told everyone I was going to Todo Santos for time to grieve and recuperate from losing my sister. Everyone was sympathetic and understanding. I bought tickets, rented a place to stay, but it was just a cover. If, or when, anyone found out I hadn't gone, I'd tell them I'd been taken down by a nasty flu with fever and delirium.

The story would also include that, in my delirium and rush to make it to bed, I'd left my purse with ID and documentation in my unlocked car. While in bed for over a week, someone had stolen my purse. Then I was so weak, I struggled to heat up soup. That's why I didn't call the insurance company or police right away.

In the meantime, I had the rest of the real plan to carry out.

In San Fran, I'd buy a first class, round-trip ticket to Paris with one of the "stolen" credit cards. I'd also book an upscale apartment in the 15th. Criminals liked to fly high.

I also needed a disguise, fake ID and passport, and a

cover story for the Frenchman, something he would swallow, nothing too fancy.

From working in the criminal justice system, I knew that the more complicated a defense or prosecution, the higher the possibility of losing a case. Don't confuse jurors with facts. It pisses them off. Go with an emotional appeal or story. Same with winning the Frenchman. Appeal to his sense of being French. Establish trust and need. Maybe even desire, if I could pull that off. Keep it simple.

Unfortunately, I knew little about Gerard Duvernet. My sister met him at the Miami Business Fair. That's it. His business card said he worked for the French government in a new program called "Creative France," a force to showcase the country's economic expertise to the world. I couldn't buy a profile search of him as it would leave a trail, but I did find the program's number.

I created my alias. First name Helen after the famous White House reporter Helen Thomas. For the surname, I settled on Craig for Daniel Craig because "Spectre" was the last film Sophie and I had watched together.

After I bought a GMS burner smartphone with cash, I called a contact who owes me. Working in criminal law, I'd met all kinds. Plus I'd saved a few from a life in prison. This one owed me big time. I hated doing it, but I knew he'd keep his mouth shut. He gave me a contact in San Francisco for a passport, a press pass, and a deadly pill. The place was a dry cleaner. On my way to Paris via San Francisco, I'd use the code he'd given me, drop off a specific piece of clothing along with a shitload of money, and the necessary information for my new identity.

The next morning at eight, I called Gerard Duvernet on the burner phone.

When a secretary put me through to his number, he answered.

"Allo. Gerard Duvernet."

My mouth went dry. I hadn't expected him to answer. I hadn't expected the resonant timber in his voice. Am I really doing this?

"Allo? Gerard Duvernet," he said again.

"Bonjour," I said. "My name is ..." I almost said my real name, Angeline Porter. A rope tightened around my chest. I'd better up my game. I couldn't afford mistakes.

"My name is Helen Craig. I'm calling from the States."

I told him I'd been assigned to write a piece for *Travel World Magazine* about what it was like to vacation in Paris during the holidays. But more importantly to me, I had a contact at the *Wall Street Journal* who was interested in an article about France's new program. Could I take him to lunch or dinner over the Christmas-New Year holidays?

Yes, he would be in Paris for the holidays. Yes, he'd be happy to meet with me.

"Who are you again?" he asked.

Oh, no. He sounded unsure.

"I was at the Miami Business Fair."

"Trés bon. Ah, the Miami Business Fair. I remember."

I bet you do.

I told him I was staying in the 15th.

"Ah, that is close to me," he said.

Yes, I know.

We arranged to meet the day before Christmas Eve. He offered to make a reservation for dinner at Le Suffren, an excellent seafood restaurant. As much as I tried to ignore his French accent, I couldn't. French accents always turned me a little watery.

Christ, I was waxing cliché poetic about a man I hated.

But for the plan to go without slip-ups, I had to keep up a pretense. I had to act charming, something that didn't come naturally to me.

"Merci, Monsieur Duvernet. Merci. I'm looking forward to our dinner."

"As am I," he said with that French formality.

I smiled. *Not as much as I am, you piece of shit.*

6

The day before leaving Eugene to go to Paris, I took a thousand dollars from a stash I kept in a fake book in my library, plus three thousand from my private savings. I set lights to automatically go on and off in individual rooms at certain times to make it look as if I were home.

On the day I left, I locked the doors and looked back at the house one time. Now I had nothing. No past. No family. This would make it easier. No matter which way it went. I might make it back. I might not.

I paid cash for a taxi ride to San Francisco and checked into the Crowne Plaza Hotel at the airport.

Once there, I called the dry cleaner. "Do you dry-clean Ocelot fur coats? Oh, and Oliver recommended you." They said yes, to drop it off around noon the next day.

The next morning I took Uber into the city where I fought the Christmas shopping rush. For my disguise, I bought a blonde, natural hair, shoulder-length wig, plus makeup and new clothes. At home, I wear jeans and sweaters when not at work and pantsuits on the job. Now I purchased a pair of riding-style boots, in fashion at the moment, three dresses, a stylish raincoat, and a Rick Steves' book on Paris, all charged to my "stolen" credit card. In a department store restroom, I took over a stall and changed into my disguise.

At the dry cleaner, I gave the code, and a man whisked me into the back where I had my photo taken and gave them my info. The documents would be delivered tomorrow to my hotel.

That night, I tested out the disguise in the bar of the hotel, a hotel remodeled in "hues and textures of nature with a stylish retro decor," another popular trend. I hated trendy, but I had to admit that this hotel and the bed were comfortable. I ordered a Manhattan, my new drink for my new persona, took out pen and notebook, and in minutes, a man at the other end of the bar asked if he could buy me a drink. I politely refused. When my Manhattan came, I pushed a twenty along the bar, but the bartender said, "From the gentleman at that table." Did my blonde sister always experience this kind of attention? Being blonde seemed to be catnip to *les chats*. I told the bartender to thank him and say I'm happily married.

I opened my journal.

On the inside cover, I wrote my new name "Helen Craig."

7

The morning after arriving in Paris, I woke with swollen eyes and that half-drugged, jet-lagged hangover. Outside, horns honked, machinery clanked, and voices drifted up from below. When I looked in the mirror, yesterday's eye makeup had melted down my face. My sister would have never let that happen. Sophie once read that Stevie Nicks had always removed her makeup before bed, and Sophie followed suit.

That was my sister. Taking advice from a rock star.

I stumbled to the bathroom and removed the makeup, then made coffee and took it to the dining room where I pulled back the curtains from the French doors.

Outside, reminders of Sophie were everywhere, even here in Paris. Across Grenelle was a Biocoop, an organics store. Sophie ate only organic vegetarian, making meals from scratch while Hank and I ate frozen dinners and junk food, unless we dined out, of course. Her kitchen always looked like the set of a cooking show with utensils, pans, and surfaces for every need. She hung garlic upside down like a bouquet and grew herbs—probably dead by now—on her sill. She even stuck miniature signs in each pot with the name of the herb. I'd often teased her that she paid so much attention to life's details, she couldn't see the big picture. She tease me back, saying I often missed what was in front of my proverbial nose.

Whenever I thought of her, my chest felt crushed. I would never feel her warm, snuggly hugs, or smell her hair. I would never see her walk into my office and turn the heads of the staff. I would never hear her voice on the phone, saying, "Hey, Sis, wait 'till you hear this!" Over time, would I stop hearing her voice? Would it fade forever?

In the bedroom, I forgot why I was there. In the bathroom, I brushed my teeth. In the kitchen I checked the fridge for bottled water. Nothing. When the noise of a passing ambulance jangled my nerves, I remembered my anxiety med. From my purse's pill case, I popped one of two left in it. As I rummaged through my suitcase, I realized I'd forgotten to pack the bottle. My mouth went dry.

Had I also forgotten the pill I'd slip Gerard on New Year's, the one that would kill him? I checked the little pouch in the side pocket of my suitcase. Whew. The small off-white pill was there in a little pouch.

My stomach growled. Food. I needed food. I needed to keep myself regularly fed and take it easy on the alcohol. I had to keep up my energy and not stress out. If I was going to do what I planned to do, I had to keep a firm grip on myself. I struggled into my clothes and wig.

Once outside, I hurried to the Franprix. Shivering, I realized I'd forgotten to wear my coat. Jesus. Get it together. I had to seduce and murder someone, for Christ's sake. That's what I'd come here for, wasn't it?

While deciding what brand of coffee to buy, I was distracted with thoughts of the Frenchman. Was he a charmer who knew how to manipulate? Or a regular guy, smitten with my sister, who realized he'd made a mistake? More likely he was in it for the sex, and when he found out she was pregnant, dumped her. I'd known men at trial who could convince you of their innocence while thrusting a knife into your ribcage.

This Frenchman might as well have thrust it into Sophie's heart. Whatever her reason for killing herself, he was to blame. I might never find out exactly what happened, but I'd try. After administering the poison to Gerard, I would have a few minutes to pump him for a confession. Maybe he'd tell me. Maybe not. It didn't matter. Justice would be served.

I grabbed a bottle of scotch, paid for my purchases, and headed back.

At the apartment, I made coffee again, ate a slice of baguette with butter, added a few slices of salami, turned on the TV, turned off the TV, paced, and paced some more.

At the dining room table, I faced the meager contents of my file on Gerard, and this time I added a photo of Sophie and me. Headed to a New Year's fête, Sophie wore a stunning bright white dress with that dazzling blond hair falling on her shoulders. She grinned, her eyes sparkled, her heart-shaped face perfection. She was engaged to a fun-loving "adventurer" who told her he had business in Cambodia. Six months later, he sent her a postcard saying he was never coming back. She sold the diamond ring he'd given her to start her business.

I pressed palms against my eyelids. I'd not only lost a sister but a possible niece or nephew. It made me sad and depressed. Hank and I—both fixated on our careers—said no to children. We figured Sophie would have a family. We'd enjoy her brood. Both of us agreed—Sophie would make a terrific mother.

Lover-boy Gerard not only broke her heart, but he'd also destroyed our family.

By noon, I'd mapped out the neighborhood and had located Le Suffren where I'd meet the Frenchman at 7:00. He hadn't given me an exact address but said he lived on Avenue de la Motte-Picquet off Grenelle near the restaurant. I decided to check out his neighborhood, including the Eiffel Tower area. One thing I knew— without my pills, I needed to stay active, keep moving.

A cold, sharp wind blew up from the river. I pulled my coat around me and walked faster. The thin blue sky gave no warmth. I darted around dog shit. Cigarette butts filled gutters, apparently a result of the no smoking ban in public places. I gave my change to a Muslim woman in a niqab and abaya, prostrate on the the sidewalk, begging.

When I looked up, four soldiers holding automatic weapons passed by, startling me. Since the terrorist attacks a month ago, I'd heard that ten thousand soldiers walked Paris streets. At least I was not going to violently shoot the Frenchman. The poison would give him a quick and painless end. He should thank me for that. I took a deep breath.

In front of cafés, men arranged boxes of oysters for sale,

fresh for Christmas Eve dinner. Patisserie windows displayed les Buches de Noel. I wondered if the Frenchman's wife would wait in line for her order. Or would she be picking up cheeses and *fois gras*? When I reached the inter-section of Grenelle and La Motte-Picquet, women dressed in quilted parkas carried cloth bags full of groceries, and I wondered if one of them was her. My head ached. My stomach roiled, and not from hunger.

I hurried up Avenue de la Motte-Picquet, trying to outrun my thoughts. Why hadn't Sophie confided in me that night? Had I said something to hurt her or make her believe I didn't care? And why had she changed her pass-words on her phone and laptop? That was strange. She always wanted me to have access to her computer or phone in case something *did* happen. After the autopsy came back, I learned Sophie had been pregnant. The final report stated, "Suicide. Motive unknown."

I was furious and called Sargent Cain to read him the report. "Motive?" I asked. "It makes it sound as if Sophie committed a crime."

Cain said, "She killed herself and a four-month fetus."

I'd forgotten his religious views. No use talking to him.

I stopped walking. I forgot where I was going. The noise in my head was throwing me off target. Oh, yes. Now I remembered. The Frenchman lived up here somewhere, probably in some swank apartment, but I had no idea where. I needed some grounding, so I turned around and walked back a few blocks to Café Desaix where I grabbed a table in the glass-enclosed smoking area. A few tables away, a couple shared a cigarette, their knees touching, his hand caressing hers. I wished Hank were here. Putting away a rapist was one thing. Murder was something entirely differ-ent. I pulled out my journal.

My hand shook as I fumbled in my purse for pen and journal. I ordered coffee, a crepe, and scotch in my rusty French. The waiter said, "Very good, Madame. Is that all?" He spoke English. *Naturellement.*

What was I doing here? Was I really going to do what I'd come here to do? Would Sophie want me to?

Across the street, I thought I saw her. I called her name. It came out garbled. I waved frantically. I tried again. She turned her head slightly. The woman picked up a department store bag filled with toys and walked away.

This corner café table suited me. I could watch people come and go with a minimum of interference. I ordered a second scotch and knocked it back. I had to call Gerard. I had to hear his voice. I had to make this real. When his voicemail answered, I struggled to keep my voice level. "This is Helen Craig. I'm looking forward to dinner tonight, my treat, of course. See you at seven." I hung up.

It wasn't enough.

On a paper napkin I wrote, "Kill the bastard," then I shredded it. The *maître d'* seated two young women next to me, their features so similar, they had to be sisters. I swallowed a sob.

The crepe came. I ate without tasting it. When the food settled, my blood flowed again. Only then was I calm enough to make a list of places my fake article could cover.

Carousels—2 near the Eiffel Tower; free

Marais—shopping area and famous Le BHV Marais department store

Catacombs—the interred bones of six million Parisians

Opéra Garnier—

I stopped, pen hovering. *Opéra Garnier.* The setting for *Phantom of the Opera,* Sophie's favorite musical.

She had loved Phantom so much she saw it three times, twice in New York City and once in L.A. I wasn't big on musicals, but one night ... and now that I thought of it ... a few nights after Sophie returned from the Miami Business Fair, she insisted on watching the film version with me. Hank was gone again, so we ordered pizza, half combo, half vegetarian, drank a couple of Coronas with lime wedges, and finished off a pint of Ben and Jerry's Cherry Garcia ice cream.

The movie was sappy, overacted, nothing more than a soap opera with singing. Sophie had opinions too, but hers centered on the chandelier scene. She told me the scene came from an actual incident. In 1896 in the opera house theater, one of the counterweights of the seven-ton chandelier had broken through the ceiling and killed a construction worker. In *The Phantom*, the romanticized scene showed the chandelier falling and killing an audience member.

"It's a pivotal scene at the end of the first act in the Broadway musical," Sophie had said. "But moving the scene to the climax of the movie was a mistake. The filmmakers probably did it for effect. In my opinion, it ruins the scene's significance."

At the time, I hadn't asked "What significance?" because

I didn't care emotionally about anyone in the musical. Instead, I asked, "Did the family sue?" trying to be funny.

Sophie either didn't hear or ignored me. "It's such a romantic story."

I wanted to say, "It's a fucking tragedy, Sophie!" but didn't.

I shook off the memory, put a star next to Opera Garnier, thinking the place would be of interest to the readers for the pure opulence, and continued with my list.

Château de Vaux le Vicomte—lavishly decorated for Christmas; designed by the architect of Versailles. Definitely.

Eiffel Tower at New Years—end of the holiday season

The Eiffel Tower at New Years. Now I was thinking like a real journalist. What an ending to an article celebrating Paris life, especially after the November Paris terrorist attacks. People celebrating, drinking champagne, and partying. A thick, tipsy crowd that. ...

... that wouldn't care if a man passed out on the grass or a bench, a champagne bottle beside him.

What a perfect situation. What a perfect time and place to kill Gerard.

That night, I headed out early, the Metro casting flickering light, cold air whipping up my dress. A man stood at the corner looking me up and down. He was so obvious I glared at him as I passed. Was this what Sophie had experienced all her life? Of course, she had. But Sophie was so unaffected by this type of attention.

By the time I reached Suffren, I couldn't feel my feet, and I rubbed my hands together. The maître d' helped remove my coat and seated me. The restaurant hummed, and with most Paris restaurants, the tables stood close together and bottles of wine bloomed everywhere. I asked for a glass of Merlot, leaving the rest of the wine choices to the Frenchman.

I drank slowly. When Gerard walked in, I recognized him immediately, and something happened I didn't expect —my body overheated and my heart raced, not from anxiety. He had what I could only call charisma. Some nondefinable characteristic that sent signals to my lower parts. I patted the perspiration from my neck and forehead. I tried to breathe sense into my traitorous body. This could not happen. I could not be attracted to the bastard.

He caught my eye just before the maître d' welcomed him like an old friend. I set the wine glass down, my hand trembling. Jesus. This was my sister's murderer. The father of her unborn child. My fists tightened. *Snap out of it, Ang. Now.*

The wine wasn't helping. I shouldn't be drinking.

I took a deep breath and inventoried him, hoping to squash my insane reaction.

Gerard was tall and immaculately dressed, classic style, nothing showy. Not Sophie's style. More my style. I grabbed my water glass. When he approached the table, I suddenly smelled the tang of wine, the shellfish platters, warm crusty bread, even the perfume of the woman next to me. I looked up. He smiled down at me, tanned face, brown eyes, strong chin, not weak like in his photo. He held out his hand. I shook it. He held mine for an extra moment. My heart raced.

I hardly remembered the first part of the evening, the polite chitchat, the seafood platter that Gerard ordered. I recognized crab, oysters, mussels, prawns. He identified the rest—whelks, periwinkles, cockles, even pointing out the difference between the Papillons oysters and Fine de Claires. I watched him take a pin from a wine cork on the platter, tease the meat from the whelk shell, and pop it into his mouth.

I'd been to dinner with many men—lawyers, police, politicians, even a judge—some of them powerful, some captivating. None made my body override my mind.

I grabbed my journal and a pen from my bag and forced myself to focus. "So, Gerard, tell me about your job with the economic outreach program." Thankfully, my time in the courtroom paid off. My voice was solid, no quaver.

He enthusiastically launched into what sounded less of an advertisement and more like a passion. He was an economist. He was trying to change France's lackluster reputation as a place to do business. He wanted the world to know about France's vibrant economic future and what the country offered. As he gave details and examples, I used the shorthand I'd learned years ago and scribbled, *And what about Sophie's vibrant future? Did you ever think about that?* Then a thought occurred to me. I wrote: *Does he even know Sophie is dead?*

I scrutinized his face, watching how animatedly he spoke about the program and France, while my mind whipped through this new possibility.

Had Sophie sent him a suicide letter or email, telling him why she was doing it? Had she told him about the pregnancy? But what if she hadn't known she was pregnant?

This was new. I'd never considered it. I'd assumed Sophie knew. Suddenly I doubted it. Sophie might kill herself, but never the life inside her. She was the type who would have had the baby on her own and poured all her love into the child. So if Sophie hadn't known and had killed herself because of this bastard across the table from me, she would have never faulted him, only herself. She would accept responsibility for her choices. She just never learned from them. Shit. I'd lost touch with who my sister was because I was so intent on revenge.

"Am I talking too fast?" Gerard said.

I snapped to attention. "No, no, just fine, go on." I met his eyes and saw no pain there. What a cold bastard. Handsome, charming, but cold. Easier to kill him, I guess.

He sipped his wine and raised an eyebrow. "Why don't we leave the rest of this for another time. Over coffee perhaps? Let's enjoy our meal. I'd like to know more about you." He leaned forward. "Tell me about your travel article." His brown eyes sparkled, and he had tiny laugh lines at the corners.

I sipped my wine. Screw it. I fully understood Gerard's appeal, but I had it wrong. He wasn't a cold bastard. He was no charmer. He was what Hank called a "Boy Scout," someone genuine, idealistic, and gung-ho, characteristics I rarely ran into in my line of work. But Hank did, being a bit of a Boy Scout himself.

"I'll send you the packet of materials that will give you history and background on our mission, our goals. It's a lot to take in in one evening."

"Thank you. I appreciate that."

He borrowed my pen, wrote something on his business card, and slid it across the table. "That's my mobile number." He smiled, ordered another bottle of wine. "So what made you want to write an article about Paris during the holidays?"

Not good. Sweat beaded between my breasts, and I felt all fluttery again. He held my gaze, eager, attentive. Damn. I looked down at my journal, and my blonde hair fell forward. Jesus. I'd forgotten I was a blonde. What the hell was wrong with me? I was playing a part, I was a professional journalist, and I needed to act like one.

My heart slowed. I could do this. I sipped my wine and said, "I want readers to know what it's like to be Parisian during the holidays. How do you celebrate? What do you do Christmas Eve and Day? What do you eat? What's important to you? What's different? What's special about Paris in December? Are there any places in Paris that are of particular interest to visitors during the holidays?"

All of this came out as if I'd been thinking about the damn article for months. Gerard didn't say anything. His half-grin was disarming.

I added, "And what does Paris offer for romantic holiday places?"

"Hmmm," he said. The "hmmm" vibrated sexily in his throat. This rattled me. He asked, "Would you like coffee?"

His reaction threw me. Why? I nodded yes to the coffee. Had this disguise put me too much in my sister's shoes? Then he startled me with, "Would you like me to recommend a few places? I can accompany you if you'd like. I do have special privileges."

I jerked out of my sister's shoes and back into my own. The waiter had taken away the seafood and empty wine bottle. I wondered how a married man, with a son, could manage to break away during the holidays? I shouldn't muse. He'd managed to break away to be with Sophie.

My ultimate goal was to be with him at the Eiffel Tower for New Years. That would be the perfect place, time and crowded conditions. It was a long shot, but I was encouraged now.

"I'd appreciate recommendations."

His intense gaze made me bristle. Was he flirting? Maybe what appeared to be a "Boy Scout" exterior was really a cover for a serial cheater. I referred to my journal. "Let me read you the list of places I'm interested in and might include in the article." I didn't hurry, more to slow my mind than to engage him.

When I finished, he said, "Ah! Château de Vaux le Vicomte. Excellent. Beautiful this time of year. The Opéra Garnier, of course. We should also ride the great Ferris wheel, *La grand Roue*."

We?

He smiled. Had I said that aloud? I looked away, picked up my pen and wrote "The Great Ferris wheel."

"Where is *La grand Roue*?" I asked.

"At Place de la Concorde. Ah, I just remembered. The Jeu de Paume gallery is showing a Halsman exhibit. Would you be interested in viewing his photography?"

Was this a setup? Was I naïve in thinking he didn't know who I was? Why was he so generous with his time? I decided to test him. "Yes, that would be lovely. I've seen the photos of Marilyn Monroe along the Metro. They remind me of my sister."

I watched him and held my breath.

He didn't flinch. Maybe he didn't equate my sister with the actress. Wouldn't all men react if they heard I had a sister who looked like Marilyn Monroe?

Instead, he said, "Then your sister must look very much like you." Before I could react or even process this statement —because it was a statement, said more like a fact with no smile, no flirtation—he continued. "We can view the exhibit and then ride the Ferris wheel." He sipped his coffee. "If the weather is good, you can take excellent photos from the top."

The sister statement flummoxed me. His invitation hung between us. Who *was* this guy?

I sipped my coffee and over the edge of the cup said, "I think I'd like to end the piece with New Years at the Eiffel Tower."

I set my coffee down, picked up my pen, scratched something nonsensical into the journal, and tapped the pen against my teeth. When his silence made me nervous, I glanced up. His intensity made me squirm. I gave him a quizzical look, hoping to break the lock he seems to have on me. He looked as if he was making up his mind to ... what?

I reached for extra sugar for my coffee, and my fingers accidentally brushed his hand. We caught each other's eyes. He immediately relaxed and said, "I'd be happy to accompany you on New Years to Madame Eiffel."

The offer sounded so formal using the Parisian "Madame Eiffel" that I almost laughed. But I also felt a tremor of excitement and ... heat.

Suddenly I smelled Sophie's perfume, and before I could stop, I blurted out, "What about your wife and son?"

He set his cup down, leaned back, and looked at me. Puzzled? Suspicious?

"What makes you think I am married?"

Was he messing with me? I let my genuine surprise show. "You aren't? I thought my contact said you were." I forced a smile. "*C'est faux pas. Désolé.*"

I expected him to say, *No faux pas. I am married, and I have a little boy named Paul.*

Instead, he said, "I have never been married."

Now he appeared slightly bemused. Not married?

The restaurant grew noisy with children's shrill voices, couples conversing, cutlery clinking. A glass shattered. Beyond the restaurant, the street appeared flat and deserted. Now what? I didn't know what to make of this. Maybe he'd told Sophie he was married so she wouldn't expect a future with him. Maybe it had been an effective way to keep her a mistress and not have any obligations. Whatever it was, I was of two minds: *The fucking asshole!* And, *Oh, my God, he's single.*

Then I reminded myself that I was *not* Helen Craig, single American journalist. I was Angeline Porter, married, former criminal lawyer, here to exact revenge.

I fumbled a thank you, another apology, as he called for a taxi to take me back to the apartment. Outside on the sidewalk, delicate arches of tiny white lights hung above the dark street. I clutched my purse to my chest. Before the taxi arrived, we arranged to meet the next day to visit the Catacombs.

11

We met at the Catacombs entrance at 9:30. Gerard had purchased tickets for a 10:00 entry. A line of frustrated tourists wound around the block.

I was more conflicted than ever about spending time with him. Last night in bed, I'd pinched myself hard, over and over, for having any attraction to him. Maybe it was the wine, or the glass of scotch I'd slugged back after the taxi dropped me off. I'd been tired, wound up. Plotting to kill him, for God's sake. I'd tried to tell myself that my attraction was just a way of understanding their affair and my sister's love for the man. But that was bullshit.

As we waited in line, the chemistry only grew. So did the mystery. Not married? No child? I poked around about his visits to the States. Maybe he'd slip and divulge a trip or two to Oregon.

But in our half hour of conversation, he talked mostly about one trip to Washington, D.C. and two to New York City. I lost focus. We were silent as we entered the Catacombs, descended 130 circular steps. How easy it would have been to push him, to watch him fall down those stone stairs. Instead, we bumped into each other at intervals, and I had an impulse to grab his hand. I didn't.

He continued to talk about the Catacombs, an ossuary, the correct term for any place where the bones of the dead were placed. He explained that the Paris cemeteries by the 1700s had become overcrowded, a health hazard, and needed to have something done. At the same time, the once active limestone quarries beneath the city had been abandoned, creating massive sinkholes in parts of Paris. Gerard said, "It appeals to me that Parisians hold up our city."

This pissed me off. I wanted to say, "You didn't hold up my sister, you gutless fuck."

Instead, I said, "Really? I bet it had nothing to do with health hazards or holding up the city. I'll bet the Catholic churches wanted to evacuate the cemeteries because they saw a windfall of valuable real estate."

He didn't respond. In fact, his tanned face darkened. As we walked down a corridor, silence ensued until we reached them—the bones of six million people.

The femurs and skulls of the very long departed were carefully and, at times, artfully arranged. I could imagine Sophie pointing out details. "Oh, look, Ang. Those small skulls. You know they were children. And this one? Oh, my god. There's a gunshot hole in this one. This is all too sad."

Yes, Sophie. This *was* all too sad.

Gerard stopped and turned. He looked concerned. "Should we leave?"

I shook my head as I stared at skulls arranged in the shape of a heart. "No, I'm fine. Continue."

Thankfully, when I returned home, an urn with Sophie's ashes would be delivered to the house. I'd seen ashes before, knew what they were like. I would sit on the couch and run my fingers through what once was my sister, a mix of ash, grit, and pieces of bone. I would do this to remember her, to let her know that I still loved her, that she might only be ashes, but she was alive in my mind and heart.

No one would put her bones up for viewing.

12

We exited to an alley far from the Catacombs' entrance and found a display map to the nearby Metros. While I tried to get my bearings, Gerard said, "What are you doing for Christmas Eve? Would you like to have dinner with a few friends and me?"

Oh, god, no. The less I knew about Gerard, the better. I couldn't off a guy after meeting his friends, especially on Christmas Eve. I had limits. His invitation, however, was hard to turn down. I couldn't deny the sex appeal of this murdering son of a bitch. He waited patiently and nervously for my answer. What excuse could I use to refuse?

Before I could answer, two beautiful women walked over and asked something of Gerard in French that I didn't understand. They carried on a lively conversation, leaving me forgotten on the cobblestones. There was no mistaking *their* flirtation, or *his*. Had he ignored Sophie like this too?

I left. Halfway down the alley, Gerard caught up with me and took my arm. "Helen?" He smiled. Bastard. Sophie deserved better. Quickly, I recognized a Metro entrance, slipped from his arm, and rushed off without a goodbye or thank you.

13

On Christmas Day, I took to the streets, unable to sit still. Under a cloudy, sullen day, I walked. And walked. And walked. I'd really blown it. The Frenchman had handed me New Year's Eve, and now he'd never speak to me again. Why had I acted that way? I was a fool. Jealousy had ruined my plans. So what if he'd flirted? I was married.

The heaviness of the day and my mood forced me to a bench in a park near the Eiffel Tower. I watched a group of tatted, punk style, twenty-somethings smoke cigarettes and pass around chips and a bottle. *They* seemed happy.

Along the Eiffel Tower, I wandered among a dozen or more kiosks of takeaway food, colorful clothing, and souvenirs, then passed a small frozen pond where children happily skated and squealed with delight. Sophie's suicide didn't make sense. She'd loved children. If the Frenchman dumped her because she was pregnant, she would have come to Hank and me. We would have helped. She knew that, didn't she? So she couldn't have known about the pregnancy. No way. In fact, maybe her crazy hormones pushed her to suicide. Yes. That made more sense.

I spent the rest of the day walking and wondering what to do next. I needed to get Gerard back on the hook. But how? I wished I had my meds. The physical exercise helped a little, but my anxiety was so high, I hadn't paid attention and had walked so far away from the apartment that I took the Metro back.

At the apartment, I took a shower and ate cheese and baguette slices, my mainstay. When my cell rang, I jumped. Who had this number? Breathless, I looked at the ID. Gerard. Now I knew I was out of control. Of course. I'd called him from the burner phone. I hesitated too long, and the ringing stopped. A few seconds later, the phone buzzed with a voicemail.

"Allo, Helen. I hope you're all right. You left so suddenly yesterday." He paused. "Would you like to meet me for a drink today? I know a few places that are open on Christmas." He hesitated. "Are you free tomorrow? I can arrange a tour of the Château de Vaux le Vicomte if you're still interested. I think this could be the centerpiece of your article. The Château remains decorated for Christmas and very romantic. I await your call."

14

I remembered seeing *Thelma and Louise* with Sophie, how angry we both were that the women had ended up acting like men and driven their car off a cliff instead of being taken by the law. "That's a feminist movie?" she'd shouted as we left the theater. "We don't need to kill ourselves to escape a misogynistic world. That's just bullshit."

Yes, it was bullshit. So why'd you do it, Sophie?

15

The Frenchman picked me up at the corner of Desaix and Grenelle in his blue Peugeot and drove the thirty-four miles through the French countryside, all the while telling me about the Baroque 17th-century chateau, a forerunner of Versailles, with its optical illusion of a massive formal garden. How Nicolas Fouquet the owner, King Louis XIV's superintendent of finances, had to demolish three villages to build the place. Then Fouquet, because the king was jealous of the chateau and Fouquet's grand, lavish fetes, was imprisoned for the rest of his life.

I said something droll, like, "The unfairness of life."

Gerard laughed.

The chateau was everything a chateau should be and more. Again, Gerard showed ID, and we skirted around the mass of people standing in line for entry. Once past the service building, I stopped for a moment, taking in the beautifully designed chateau with its moat and bridge, the formal gardens, its gorgeous backdrop.

Inside, Christmas was everywhere. Tiny lights for candles and fireplace garlands, Christmas trees with themed decorations in each room, the first with artificial snow, antique blue decorations, angels. Gerard followed. The crowds pushed us ever closer. I could almost feel his breath on my neck, making his nearness unbearable. I hurried to the next room with its all-white decorations. Angels, owls, teddy bears, ribbons, and doves. A white rabbit beneath the tree, tall white angels with wings spread.

Tapestries, chandeliers, statues, paintings, vaulted Sistine Chapel-style ceilings filled the rooms. Each room had its own story told on a plaque nearby. But I couldn't concentrate enough to read, not with Gerard right behind me.

He said, "Eighteen thousand people were once employed to keep this place running." I turned to look at him and, as I thought about those lips kissing me, said to myself, *I bet he didn't say things like that when he was screwing my sister in some fancy hotel room.*

I darted off to the last room before the bedrooms and drew to an abrupt halt. A room for children. Red, green and blue stars sparkled on white giraffes. Toadstools. Clowns of all sizes dressed in red and blue. Four trees decorated with big bows, shiny and sparkling, silver moons, tiny clowns, and presents beneath. Carousel-type horses. Hula-hoops. Sophie had been a hula-hoop queen. I remembered.

When Gerard took my arm, I let go an angry exhale, wrenched free, and pushed through the crowd, past a minia-ture working Ferris wheel, down stone stairs, through the underground passages lined with wine barrels and into the servants' kitchen where a taxidermist boar lay on a thick table.

Finally, outside, I was at the top of stone stairs, looking toward the horizon, the perspective of the pools causing a surreal view of the great gardens. I was breathing so hard a woman with her daughter asked if I was all right. I said, "Oui. Merci." Gerard drew up next to me.

"It's astounding to think Fouquet was only twenty-six when he started the chateau," he said.

Was that all he could think about? The damned chateau?

"Silicon Valley millionaires are younger than that," I said, my voice not hiding its disdain for his French entitlement and obliviousness to my pain. I added, "My sister wouldn't be caught dead visiting this place."

"Are you OK?" he asked, drawing nearer. "Is something wrong?" He took my hand. I froze, but I didn't pull away. It felt so good to have human contact, human kindness.

What the hell was I doing? I must be mad. But when I glanced at him, the sun lit up the delicate hairs on his neck. He looked genuinely concerned for me.

I turned away. "My sister died not long ago. I miss her, that's all." Tears rolled down my face.

His hand gripped mine tightly, almost painfully. I glanced up. He looked genuinely stricken. He pulled me to him, wrapped his arms around me, and rested his head on my shoulder. "*Je suis tellement désolé,*" he whispered. He didn't have to translate.

He held me for much longer than he should have. When I broke away, Gerard gave me his hankie to wipe my face, even though his eyes filled with tears, too.

God, I was so fucked.

I said, "I'd like to leave now."

16

W
e were silent on the way back. He probably thought I was crazy. But then again, the French were used to public displays of emotion, weren't they? I wasn't angry anymore, just broken-hearted and bereft. I almost confessed to Gerard why I was in Paris, but that would have been crazy.

As we entered the city, he said, "Would it help you to talk about your sister, your anguish?"

Anguish? I said nothing.

"I feel as if we've known each other before."

My nails dug into my palms. Known each other before? Was he serious? Did he finally see Sophie in my face?

In a neutral voice, I said, "You don't know me, and you never will."

Suddenly, he looked as if he'd aged ten years. Good. He had destroyed Sophie. I was too angry to make nice. Maybe I could call him later and lean on his sympathies, but I sure as hell couldn't talk to him about my sister. Bastard.

When he dropped me off a few blocks from the apartment, I said, "Thanks," and walked away. He didn't try to stop me. He didn't call me back. Shit. What in hell had possessed me to mention Sophie to him? Stupid. Stupid. Stupid. I'd probably blown it for good this time.

17

The following day I played solitaire in an attempt to pass the time and stop thinking. After hours of never winning a game, I realized the Jack of Hearts was missing.

Sophie would have teased me about not playing with a full deck. How could I have played that long and not noticed? Then I reminded myself—I was not taking my meds.

I needed air, had to get out of the apartment.

I slipped into my disguise and set out to the Jeu de Paume and the Halsman exhibit. I lose myself in museums and galleries, spending hours listening to audio guides. Hank would always sweep through. Even on our first trip to Paris, he had sped through the Louvre, bought coffee somewhere, read the paper, and waited for me on the Pont des Arts watching private boats, *bateaux mouches*, and houseboats on the Seine. He'd never rushed me. How had I lucked out with love while Sophie had always struggled?

At the Jeu de Paume, I passed through the security system and headed upstairs to the Halsman "Astonish Me!"

exhibit. I was beyond wanting to be "astonished." All I wanted was to stare at photos of Marilyn Monroe as if I could call forth Sophie's spirit and bring her back to life.

But who was I kidding? Marilyn hadn't even been able to save herself.

Soon I found Halsman's "jumpology" shots, photos of celebrities jumping, poses that he considered "disinhibiting," the act of jumping "took off the mask." In Marilyn's jump shots, she looked more frightened than disinhibited, except for when Halsman jumped with her. In the last frame, she finally appeared to be having fun. Maybe the human contact of holding his hand had helped. I tried to picture Gerard and Sophie holding hands and jumping, laughing. Instead, I imagined his hand on her breast, her ass, helping her in and out of a taxi. I shook away the image. I wanted to think of him spoiling her a little. She'd deserved to be spoiled.

Then I noticed the contact sheet of Marilyn's first shoot for *Life Magazine* before she had work done and years before her entanglement with the Kennedys. Her long, wavy hair fell around her baby cheeks and smiling face. I stopped and stepped back, the fate of my sister suddenly paralleling Marilyn's. Both had died because of a lover.

Now I was livid and grief-stricken at the same time. I hugged myself, pinched my upper arms to force back tears, wishing I *had* told Hank and asked him to come home from China. Why hadn't I?

He'd once lamented how "the scumbags inherit the earth," sounding like a disgruntled character out of an old TV series. Would he have helped me plan revenge, get justice for my sister? Underneath his occasional blustering, he was the most moral man I knew. He would never condone murder for any reason.

I quickly left the exhibit. Outside rain spit on stone. As kids, Sophie and I had rolled up our jeans and stomped mud puddles in our bare feet. We'd caught frogs, spied on the neighborhood boys, and made lunches that we wrapped in kitchen towels and ate by the lake. We pretended we *were* orphans, and we were in a way. Both our mom and dad had to work long hours to stay afloat, so they relied on the neighbors to keep an eye on us. But the neighbors also had jobs, kids, and little attention left to watch us, so Sophie and I relied on each other. That had made us orphans. No one understood what that meant. Like the time a man had followed us home and tried to push his way into our house, and we screamed our fool heads off until he ran. Or the time Sophie fell off her bike, and I patched her up. No one knew what we had gone through, except each other. The Frenchman had taken my only sibling, my best friend, my fellow orphan.

On Place de la Concorde, the wind carried rain and street grime across the bricks. People huddled or scurried past, their faces covered, and I felt as if I could be in any big city anywhere in the world. With a hand to shield my eyes, I hurried toward the Ferris wheel.

I hated heights, but today didn't matter. Nothing did. Let the damn wind blow me away. I paid my twelve Euros, and because few people rode, I had a seat in a pod to myself. When the wheel stopped at the top, I clasped my heart and breathed with forceful inhales and exhales. I wanted to close my eyes, but the clouds dispersed and allowed a limited view of Champs Elysees, Eiffel Tower, Place de la Concorde, and a skyline of high-rise buildings in the far distance. I didn't look down to the sidewalks. Only up.

Sophie and I had talked about taking trips together—to Paris, Venice. Sophie had wanted to go to Hawaii. Now we'd never get the chance. The finality of it caused a gut punch. I shut my eyes and reached beside me, felt her small, warm and familiar hand in mine. "He won't get away with this, Soph. He won't hurt anyone ever again." When I said this, the wheel began to turn again. Her hand was gone.

18

At the apartment, I poured three fingers of scotch. I had no idea what to do next, but once the liquid courage hit, I knew I had to call Gerard and apologize. He answered. I didn't get past a greeting before he said, "I can't stop thinking about you. I'm so sorry about your sister. If anything was my fault the other day, I hope you'll forgive me." He sounded so sincere. "Can we have a glass of wine or meet for coffee? I really think we—"

"Yes. Yes, of course. But not tonight."

I didn't want to be alone with him. No coffee or dinner. I couldn't trust myself around him. When I was away from him, I hated him. When I was near him. ... I needed to keep it professional. I arranged to meet him at the opera house the next day.

19

I arrived early, paid the entrance fee, and waited in the mirrored, gothic rotunda of the opera house where the guided tours started. When the Frenchman walked in, he looked around for me.

God. No wonder Sophie had fallen for him. He turned heads, although he seemed oblivious to it, like Hank. Some men who went to prison had magnetism too. Maybe it was self-assurance. Maybe they'd been told all their lives they were sexy. Maybe they had more pheromones. I applied lipstick for the third time. How did women keep this on all day? My dress felt too tight and the bench too hard. I pushed back my shoulders and tried to relax, but my foot tapped the floor uncontrollably.

Finally, he saw me, walked over, and broke into a smile. "Thank you for joining me."

"Of course," I said a bit too loudly. I withdrew pen and notebook and found a blank page. "Do you know much about the opera house?"

I remained formal. He told me the ballet was housed here and he held season tickets. The opera itself had long since moved to a different venue. "Would you like to see the grotto? I could arrange a tour on another day if that interests you."

I wondered if Sophie had told him about her love of *Phantom of the Opera*. What perfect justice to kill Sophie's lover in the grotto. But that didn't fit my plan.

"Perhaps another time," I said. So with that, Gerard led me into the building.

We moved through and around throngs of people. Like a dance partner, he lightly placed his hand on my back to guide me, and I shivered. I heard bits of what Gerard said. "...built from 1861-1875 ... nineteen hundred seats ... Second-Empire Beaux-Arts style ... a showcase for the rich." Halfway up the Grand Escalier, the ceremonial staircase, we paused and turned to look back. In a demonstration, he said, "Here the man would stop. ..." He held out his arm. "... and the woman would place her hand on his extended forearm and show her finery to those below." He took my hand and placed it on his forearm. I wore a tight, finely knit wool dress, pale yellow, and I noticed his appraising glance. I withdrew my hand and proceeded up the staircase, my stomach a mess.

At the theater door, a security guard checked my passport. An Israeli company was setting up a ballet. Someone shouted orders to stagehands. A tour filed into seats. Gerard showed his ID as he had before, and we took two seats near the front and away from the group. I could feel his body warmth and smell evaporated rain on his clothing. He told me about the theater. I wrote a few shorthand notes in my journal, trying not to notice his hand so close to my thigh. I looked up and caught his eye. He grazed my leg with the back of his hand, and I bit my lip. I wanted to run my fingers through that thick dark hair, over his arched eyebrow, down to those lips I imagined on mine. I had to stop, but I didn't want to. I leaned into him.

He turned, pulled me to him, and kissed me.

Our position was so awkward our lips didn't fully meet. A woman sitting a few rows behind us cleared her throat, but Gerard turned slightly and reached across my shoulders, pulling me closer. He tasted of coffee and smelled of lavender-scented shave cream. The more intense and demanding the kiss, the more scared I became. I didn't want this. I couldn't. A crash from the stage broke us apart.

A stagehand had dropped a prop. We both laughed with embarrassment. I straightened in my seat and opened my journal. My hands shook. "Tell me about the theater," I said, the words rushing together, my pen hovering over a page. "What about the ceiling? The Chagall? The building is so formal and Chagall is so playful."

I felt him relax. "I would also add magical. Chagall painted this in 1960, and it wasn't immediately popular. He refused to take pay for his work." Gerard cleared his throat. "I think choosing a Jew to paint this famous ceiling was an attempt to apologize for France's decades of anti-Semitism, particularly during World War II."

"Interesting," I said.

"I'm sure you've heard about the chandelier."

Now I popped to attention.

"Made of bronze and crystal, it weighs seven tons." He glanced over at me, unclasped his hands, and rested them on his thighs. "In 1896, one of the chandelier's counterweights broke free and burst through the ceiling into the auditorium, killing a construction worker. Have you seen *The Phantom of the Opera*?"

My heart banged against my chest. I nodded.

"Then you know they use a similar scene in the musical,

only the chandelier comes down and kills an audience member." I waited, holding my breath. "It's a signature moment at the end of the first act. But in the film version, they moved it to the climax of the movie. In my opinion, it ruins the scene's significance."

I stood so abruptly I almost fell.

In my opinion, it ruins the scene's significance.

My sister's *exact* words.

Gerard rose. "Helen? Are you all right?"

"I feel a bit queasy."

He took my arm and hurried us out, down halls and stairs, then through the gift shop and outside where I held my face up to a cold mist.

"Helen?" he repeated.

"I'm OK," I mumbled. Hadn't Sophie said there are no coincidences?

We walked, me hurrying ahead of him. He tried to keep up, placing his hand on my back, but I shrugged it off as we zigzagged down quiet streets, my stomach even more in turmoil. I felt his confusion. I'd given him mixed signals. Kissing one moment, running off the next. Every day with him, I did something crazy. What did he think of me? Did he like crazy?

It was quite theatrical, really, and reminded me of how I'd acted before I started taking the medication.

But so what if I was confusing him? It didn't matter. Gerard's feelings didn't matter. All that mattered was Sophie.

Abruptly, I stopped. Across the street, families gathered around the Galleries Lafayette department store animated windows. I hurried to join them. Gerard caught up with me at the Star Wars display. A five-year-old boy squealed and stomped his feet. His mama scooped him up and held him on her hip while the father approached with a baby strapped to his chest.

A baby.

Like the promise of seasons, of the sun rising and setting, I knew I would send Gerard to his afterlife.

20

I didn't remember the Metro ride back to the apartment, or the evening. Time meant nothing. Memory was no longer important.

I woke, still wearing the wig. My mouth tasted foul. My journal lay open on the dining room table, copious shorthand notes written on two pages, a big X over one. A bottle of scotch, half full, sat next to a glass and an untouched plate of crackers, cheese, and olives. On the other side was an ashtray full of cigarette butts. I was losing my grip. I'd given up smoking. I'd probably bought a pack on my return. My cell blinked with a message.

"I hope you're feeling better this morning. I share your grief upon losing your sister. Do you still plan on sharing New Years with me?"

You bet your ass I was.

I called him. We arranged to have a light dinner at a nearby café and then walk to the Seine and Eiffel around 10:30 to join the rest of the revelers.

I prepared, buying a very nice bottle of champagne,

champagne glasses, napkins, brie, and crackers, along with a shoulder tote to carry them. The tote had a convenient small pocket on the inside, a pocket that would hold the carefully wrapped pill that would kill Gerard.

21

Over the next few days, I shopped. I bought a tight, cherry-red, sexy dress. The woman who sold it to me said it had "excellent décolletage." She also recommended gold flats for more comfortable walking and a scarf of gold, black and red that complimented the ensemble. Hank would spit out his burger if he saw me in this. Unfortunately, he wouldn't. I had to throw it away before going home.

On New Year's Eve day, I spent extra time on the wig and makeup, slipped small gold hoops into my ears, and downed some scotch, not too much, just enough to take the edge off. I was drinking too much, forgetting too much. I wondered how I'd live with myself after murdering Gerard. Still, I'd been around murderers. A few had been perfectly rational about what they'd done, offering what I thought were good reasons for killing someone.

"He killed my brother and the cops weren't going to do anything about it."

"We ended up penniless because he wore a suit and

bilked us out of our lifetime savings. He ruined many lives. A few people committed suicide. Then the motherfucker got off scot-free. He deserved his fate."

"He abused me for years. Even with a restraining order, he found me and beat me. I lost a baby because of him. I had to protect myself."

I couldn't blame them. I sympathized. In my case, how was I expected to sit idly by when the man responsible for my sister's death, as well as her unborn child, was free to victimize someone else?

I headed out.

I met Gerard at L'Atome. We were cordial. I tried not to drink too much. I tried not to look into his eyes. My brain, however, would not slow down. My thoughts ricocheted back and forth. I found it difficult to swallow. If only this had been under different circumstances. If only my sister hadn't had an affair with him. If only he hadn't dumped her.

If only Sophie had confided in me. If only I had called her that night. If only I had discouraged her in the first place. If only, if only, if only.

When Gerard held out a piece of scallop on his fork and put it to my lips, I wanted to both suck it into my mouth and spit it at him. Our conversation lurched-stopped-started over and over again like a broken down car. After dinner, we walked to Pont de Bir-Hakeim overlooking the Seine. Police cars and vans lined Quai Branly, the street leading to the Eiffel Tower, all the way from Avenue de Suffren to Pont d'Iena where crowds flooded into the Eiffel area. I tied my scarf over my head as the wind chafed my cheeks and whipped up my dress. I was burning inside. We stared out at the river, saying nothing.

Then three French women with bottles of champagne and smartphones in hand asked Gerard to take their photo.

The women already had had more than their fair share to drink, and they flirted outrageously with him. He flirted with them. Again. As if I were not there.

I shouldered my bag and walked away. Gerard *again* caught up with me and took my arm. I let him. I had to maintain control. All Frenchmen flirt, I reminded myself.

But this was no ordinary Frenchman.

We maneuvered through the crowd along the *quai* and stopped just before reaching the carousel across from the Eiffel. Gerard gave me a lopsided grin, something I hadn't seen before. Boyish. Adorable. Now I wished I had murdered him the first night and been done with it. He bought me a stupid, little souvenir, a silver Eiffel Tower about three inches tall. I kissed his cheek and dropped it into my bag. When he tried to kiss me, I turned away and the wind blew the scarf from my head and whipped my hair into my face. I shoved back the unfamiliar blonde strands.

The blonde hair reminded me of why I was there. Plus, it reminded me that Gerard was not attracted to me. He was attracted to Sophie. Under this vulnerable disguise, I was Angeline, thick armored and tough. I'd never tried to be sexy, just dependable and rational.

I couldn't compete with a beautiful sister like Sophie, so I didn't try. But right now I was ugly under my disguise. Maybe I'd always felt ugly.

No, it was worse. When I'd been with Sophie, I'd felt invisible.

Gerard said something, but I couldn't hear. If he touched me, I'd slug him. Had Sophie killed herself because of this guy? Really? He was sexy, but so what?

That's when I realized I was not just feeling anger. I was feeling a green-eyed, newly risen, virulent jealousy.

Of my dead sister.

Oddly, when I acknowledged this, I felt calmer, more in control. Then I realized what erupted beneath—a raging anger at Sophie. She hadn't thought about how her suicide would affect me, the loss, the pain she'd caused. She hadn't had the decency to leave me a suicide note. If she hadn't been dead, I might have killed her myself.

Gerard gestured to indicate the crowd. "I love my fellow Parisians, the mix, how different ethnicities can peacefully gather after such horrific attacks."

I nodded. Around us, champagne corks popped, bubbly flowed like any normal New Years.

I smiled at him. "I think it's time for champagne."

We opened a bottle. I poured a glass for each of us. We sipped as we walked from the carousel area to search for a place to sit. After finding a patch of grass along the embankment across from the Eiffel, he put an arm around me and my thighs traitorously tingled.

I downed another glass, and before I knew it, we'd finished the bottle. The tingling traveled up my body to my chest and head. I could smell him again. His breath was on my neck. If I was to be an avenging angel, I also needed to be the devil, feel nothing.

Fifteen minutes to midnight. We were out of champagne. Gerard pulled me to him, kissed me long and hard, my breasts against his chest, our legs awkwardly interlocked. When we pulled away, I looked for someone selling champagne.

How could I kill him? My stupid sister was to blame for this.

But I reminded myself that Sophie's choices had always seemed reasonable at first. Even after they started to go wrong, she had set her mind and was unstoppable. Gerard was no different—a man who had seduced her, made her fall in love, then left her. I might have been jealous of Sophie's beauty, but she'd always envied my marriage to Hank, of our happiness and partnership. "And the sex is still great," I had once shared.

I looked at Gerard. He was no Hank.

It was time.

But we were out of champagne. Shit. "Ok," I told myself calmly. "Ok."

Let the next ten minutes determine his fate. I relaxed a little. I was no longer in charge.

Lights flashed as a procession of police cars and vans moved from the sidewalk and up the street, crossed the bridge, turned and returned. People called out, "Vive la France!" Some sang "La Marseillaise." The crowd ramped up for midnight.

Five minutes to go. A young man selling champagne from a backpack approached us, and Gerard paid an extraordinary amount for a mediocre bottle. He opened the bottle and filled our glasses. I placed the half-empty bottle in the tote bag. Fate had stepped in. Now I needed to go through with it.

Gerard put his arm around me. "Are you cold?"

I shook my head and tried to smile. We drank.

A group of young Parisians filled in the open spots around us. The crowd became more raucous waiting for the Eiffel Tower to light up. Blood pounded in my ears. It was happening too fast.

One minute to midnight.

I fiddled with my shoulder bag, slipped the pill from the packet into my hand. While Gerard watched the police caravan proceed up the *quai* and across the bridge, I took his glass, dropped in the pill, refilled the glass, and handed it to him. I filled my glass. We waited to toast the New Year.

I kept my focus on the street across from us.

He picked up a lock of my hair. "You look beautiful tonight."

Why couldn't he tell it was a wig?

I glanced at his glass. I could knock it out of his hand. I could ask him all those questions I needed answers to: why did you betray my sister? If you're single, why did you lie? Why couldn't you love her? Why did you have to be like all the others?

Damn him.

Midnight struck.

The cheering drowned out the pounding in my chest. The Eiffel Tower lit up in red, white and blue. White balloons ascended to the sky. When I turned to him, his glass was empty. I froze.

He reached for my hand.

Oh, god. I'd done it. Tears welled. As much as I hated him, I wanted him to live. I was crazy. I was beyond redemption.

He acted normal. Why wasn't he feeling it?

As people continued to shout and cheer, I whispered, "Sophie, Sophie, Sophie," my mantra. He turned to kiss me.

I shook my head and said, "Why?"

More singing. More cheering, kissing, clapping. Everyone was happy. Parisians had made it through another year.

Suddenly Gerard looked at me with a puzzled expression.

Everything I'd wanted to ask him floated away as I reminded myself that I'd had no choice. I'd done what had to be done. Justice for Sophie.

His expression changed. It chilled me to the bone. He

looked like a little boy, punished for something he didn't understand.

"Helen?" he whispered. Pain spread across his face.

Suddenly I was overwhelmed with the smell of sweat, sparklers, alcohol, perfume, cigarette smoke. I was going to vomit. He dropped his plastic glass down the embankment. His body convulsed. His skin paled. I grabbed his hand. "I'm sorry. I'm so sorry." He tried to speak but couldn't. "My sister Sophie. Remember her?" Now he looked scared. "She hung herself."

No one paid any attention to us.

He managed to squeak out, "Qu ... uoi...?" then stared at me, wide-eyed and frightened. His eyes lost their focus and his eyelids fluttered. A dribble of foam trickled from the corner of his mouth before he toppled to the side, his head landing in my lap.

People packed up to leave or toasted with more champagne. I slid from beneath him, scrambled to my feet, and grabbed the tote bag.

I forced myself to walk normally. When I reached the end of the *quai*, I headed up Grenelle amidst a crowd of people. I had to get rid of the bag. Ahead, I saw a trash bin and was about to shove the bag into it when I looked up at the Santa I'd seen the day I arrived in Paris. His suit had become a dirty bag hanging from his body, but his eyes narrowed, and he pointed a drunken finger at me.

I ran, feeling his eyes on me. I ducked around the building. After I caught my breath, I peeked around the corner. He was gone.

At the apartment, I could barely get the key into the lock. Inside, my chest hurt so badly and my heart banged so hard, I thought it was a heart attack. I threw the bag on the couch and took in one rattled breath after another until the shaking stopped. Over and over I told myself now was not the time to second-guess myself. I'd done it. Finally, when my legs moved, I made my way to the table and sat down. I shoved all my notes and files into a pile to take to the trash and decided this never happened.

22

I threw the bag and contents of my suitcase into two separate Metro station bins and gave my carryon to a homeless woman. At the San Francisco airport, I smashed my burner phone in a cubicle in the bathroom.

At home, the house felt cold and uninhabited. I turned up the heat, took one of my meds and a sleeping pill, and slipped into bed.

When I woke, I felt as if I'd just had a long horrible nightmare. I drank my coffee and listened to messages. A few from work welcomed me back from Todo Santos, not knowing that I'd never gone. Two from Hank as he worked his way to Hong Kong and soon, in a week, home, this time to stay for a while.

There were three messages from the mortuary. The urn was ready to be delivered as I'd requested, and they would return her personal effects at that time. When would delivery be convenient?

I called Police Sargent Cain. He listened as I told him I'd had to cancel my planned trip, how sick I'd been, and apologized for not telling him right away so I could file a report. I told him in a weak voice, "This morning when my brain finally unfogged, I couldn't find my purse or cell phone. I've looked everywhere. Then I noticed my car was unlocked. I've been in such a fevered state, I left the purse in the car, and now it's gone with all my valuables. They even took the quarters in the console I used for parking meters."

Sounding distraught, I'd asked him what to do. I knew the answer, but I also knew Cain liked to help a damsel in distress. Of course, there was nothing the police could do but write up a report to use with the insurance, bank, credit card, and credit report companies. He turned me over to a desk cop, and I gave that person the details.

Off the phone, I remembered Sophie's cell phone and computer. I tried the old password again, but it didn't work. Why had she changed it? Was she hiding something? Now my conspiratorial streak grabbed hold. I spun in every direction, ones I'd never anticipated. Was Gerard more than her lover? Was he more than just a national rep for his government program? Had he used her somehow? Had Sophie known? That could explain her bizarre behavior. With a different passcode, I would never see what was on her phone. Maybe Sophie hadn't wanted me to know the full extent of her dating history and communications.

I took a quick shower. It felt good not wearing the wig. I'd dumped it at the San Fran airport.

I called my insurance and reported the theft. They faxed a report I could use. I drove into town. The DMV issued me a temporary replacement driver's license. At the AT&T store, I bought a new phone. Every time I returned to the car, I could see Gerard's face as he foamed at the mouth and fell, his face frozen in surprise.

Back home, the mailman had dropped off my held mail

and with it came the mortuary's package with the blue dress. I hesitated before opening it.

My chest heaved with suppressed grief as I pulled the dress from the brown padded envelope. The material felt like silk, but you could never tell these days. It could be polyester. I'd burn it either way. Putting the dress to my nose, I smelled Sophie. Maybe I'd keep the dress. Then I noticed the tag on the neckline. I dropped the dress to my lap. What the fuck? I read the tag again. This dress wasn't from France. It was an American designer.

Sophie had told me Gerard bought the dress in Paris for their four-month anniversary. Why had she lied? She must have noticed the tag. What if she'd bought the dress and said it was from Gerard just to impress me? Maybe she and Gerard had shopped for it together in the States. But why tell me that other story? Something didn't add up.

My sister used to shop at the Nordstrom in Portland. I called them. Did they carry this designer? Yes. Could I find out who bought the dress? Could they look up the sales receipt of this dress if I gave them my name and the law firm's. I was researching a case to rule out foul play in a suicide. It had no legal impact on the store. If they could tell me who bought the dress, I'd probably be able to put this inquiry to rest. I'd give them an approximate timeline. They said they'd get back to me. I gave them Hank's fax number.

I waited, listening to Amy Winehouse, trying not to indulge in a glass of scotch.

Around 4:00, I heard the fax machine in the office. I took the blue dress into Hank's office. His old fax made grinding noises. The room smelled stale, so I opened a window. I sat at his desk, not understanding why he hadn't bought a more comfortable chair. I looked over at a photo of him, me and Sophie, taken on a night out with her old boyfriend who ran off to Cambodia. I'd often been tempted to cut him out of the photo. Fuck him and all the men who'd treated her like shit. I knocked the photo off the corner and swiped papers to the floor.

The fax machine jerked to a stop.

I didn't know why I was so scared to pick up those papers. I sweated as I looked around the office—maps on one wall, a marker board on the other filled with equations, a periodic table of the elements behind Hank's desk, a library of science books.

I swiveled toward the fax machine. Maybe I should have left it alone. Shred the papers and gone on with the story as told. I might have if Sophie hadn't changed her passwords.

Quickly, before I could change my mind, I nabbed the faxed pages, set them on the desk, and scanned the invoice. Once. Twice. A third time. Sophie's name wasn't on it. Instead, the person who had paid for the dress was Hank, my Hank.

I turned cold. I shoved my hands under my armpits. Hank? That didn't make sense. How could that be? I dropped into his chair and stared at the invoice. No mistake —Hank's name and the last four numbers of a credit card I didn't recognize.

Shaking, I tried to stand, but couldn't. Maybe he'd bought the dress so Sophie would have something new to wear for a date with the Frenchman. But he didn't know about the Frenchman. Sophie had asked me not to tell him. And now I knew why. There'd never been a Frenchman.

It was Hank.

My Hank.

My stomach heaved. I struggled to breathe.

Hank was often gone. Cell phones made it easy to fake

locations. Sophie was mysterious about the relationship whereas before she'd always told me everything.

Now it made sense why she hadn't called me that night.

Why she'd committed suicide.

My chest turned to ice. I shook violently. I'd killed an innocent man.

I had to move. I had to do something. Maybe I was wrong. My conspiratorial streak kicked back in. Maybe Sophie *had been* involved with the Frenchman, but *he* wasn't what he said he was. Maybe she'd stumbled upon his true identity, something that put her at risk, perhaps French intelligence or even worse, a saboteur who had infiltrated the French government. Maybe she'd turned to Hank for help because she hadn't wanted to scare me. But what about the blue dress?

Maybe Hank had bought it for her for a purpose. What if Hank wasn't an engineer, but a CIA operative and had used Sophie to get information from the Frenchman?

Stop it! Stop it! I knew the truth.

But I still couldn't believe it was Hank. What gnawed at me was *The Phantom of the Opera*. How could Gerard use the exact words my sister had about the use of the chandelier? That couldn't be a coincidence. That was my evidence and proved his guilt.

Then my anger and lawyer brain kicked in.

Maybe the opinion wasn't theirs alone.

Shakily, I used my phone to Google, *"In my opinion, it ruins the scene's significance."*

Up popped two reviews with the exact wording.

Sophie and Gerard's opinions were not unique. Similar ones were all over the internet.

In the living room, I picked up Sophie's phone. Did I dare? I knew her old four-number passcode was her birthdate in reverse numerical order. I swallowed hard and entered Hank's birthdate the same way. It worked. I didn't need more evidence, but I couldn't help myself. I checked her emails. Her texts. It was all there. I wiped my sweaty palms on my jeans and scrolled through their conversations.

The last message from Hank said they needed to talk, and he'd be home soon. He asked her not to say anything to me as he felt it should be him who told me about their relationship. I had no idea what or if she had erased messages. I couldn't read anymore.

In Hank's office, I pulled his whiskey from the liquor cabinet, poured a glass, and stumbled back to Hank's chair where I rocked myself and grabbed my stomach as I tried desperately not to vomit. I was cold, so very cold. I longed to be in a Paris bistro, longed to be near the Eiffel Tower once again, to look into Gerard's innocent, trusting eyes, feel his hand on my back, drink champagne and later, finally, fall into bed with him.

I downed the whiskey, watched the late afternoon darken, and leaned my forehead on the desk. Dusk turned to evening. Car lights flashed past. A dog barked.

The phone rang. I lifted my head from the desk and answered. I knew who it was. I also knew what I'd say.

"Hi, Ang," he said. "How are you?"

I tried to talk, but couldn't.

"Ang?"

I crushed the invoice for the blue dress into a ball and said, "Sophie hung herself." I paused. "She was pregnant."

His gasp at the other end was all I needed to hear.

PART II

23

I t was Tuesday, around eleven o'clock. I was waiting for Hank to return from China. The mortuary had delivered my sister's ashes, and the silver urn sat in front of me on my kitchen counter, lit a cigarette, and knocked back a shot of whiskey. The figure of the Roman goddess Diana was etched into the silver.

I said aloud to Sophie, "Diana was the goddess of the moon and the hunt. I thought it was apropos since you were quite a hunter—of a different animal."

My stomach felt like a post that cats scratched. I found a half box of crackers. When I couldn't choke one down, I spit it into the sink.

Back at the counter, I poured another shot and lifted the glass. "'Swear not by the moon, the fickle moon ... lest thy love prove likewise variable.'" I laughed. "Nailed you, Sis."

By noon I was drunk.

Two hours later, Hank arrived. The alcohol had worn off. Rain pelted my face as I strode to his taxi, holding high an umbrella. He turned to me, and I beat him over the head. "You piece of shit!" He grabbed the umbrella and pushed me into the house. We faced off across the kitchen counter and Sophie's urn.

I swayed. A cigarette, long forgotten, burned in a candy dish.

Hank was my sister's lover. Not Gerard. *Hank.* He'd caused my sister's death.

Hank dabbed a bleeding facial cut with a napkin. His hair had grown long in two months, and he had a beard. His clothes smelled sour. My teeth chattered.

"Yes. I had an affair with Sophie, but I broke it off. She was relentless, so I went to China." He looked at the blood on the napkin. "Let's get into some dry clothes before—"

"Fuck you."

Hank took off his coat and shakily draped it on the stool. He cleared his throat to say something but didn't. His eyes watered. Was this remorse? But for what? Getting caught or causing Sophie's suicide?

"When did it start? How did it start? Who started it? Were you in love? What happened?"

I wanted to ask, "How did I not know or suspect?" But I didn't. Only I could answer that.

I wanted to ask, "Am I not enough?" But the answer was obvious.

Even though I was drunk, as a lawyer, I'd been trained to wait and not press for answers.

Hank sat down and leaned on the counter, head in hands. "When you weren't here, she kept coming over. She had excuses. She insisted I needed to update my business website. She wanted to help me. She wanted to keep me company while you were gone. We got drunk one night, and she cried about some guy who. ... Damn it, Ang. I never meant to. ..."

Again, I waited. I had been my sister's confidante. Not Hank.

"I told her she should talk to you, not me." He ran a finger along the edge of the counter, his face taking on a different expression, one I recognized. Clients looked this way when they were about to divulge info they'd kept under wraps. Or when they were about to blame someone else for the crime. I straightened, prepared.

"Sophie was not who you thought she was."

Projecting blame. Typical play.

Asshole.

"She wasn't innocent or naive." He made eye contact. Intense eye contact. "Around you, that's how she acted. But she made bad choices, and they caused problems."

"I *know* she made bad choices. *You* for example."

"You don't know the half of it, Ang. The kind of danger your sister put herself in."

I stepped back, weaving a little. Did I really want to hear this ... from him? How bad could it be? Or was he lying to distract me?

"You couldn't have stopped what happened, Ang. She did things that—"

I smacked the counter. "That's bullshit, Hank. You could have told me. We could have dealt with her together."

He hesitated. "Sophie took a video of us making love— without me knowing it."

My stomach lurched. "What do you mean?"

"Ang, she said she'd show it to you if I didn't stay with her. She wanted me to get a divorce from you. Then after a safe period, we'd pretend we'd fallen in love."

"Sophie wouldn't do that!"

"That's what I'm saying. You didn't know her like you thought you did. Sophie was selfish. She wanted what you had." He glanced up at the ceiling as if measuring his next move. "She lied. A lot."

I stared, speechless. "*Lied? What* about you?"

Blood drained from his face. "We'll talk about this later. When you're sober, and I've slept." He didn't wait for my objection and headed upstairs.

I followed, shouting, "You *knew* about the pregnancy? You fucking knew? Stop, damn it! Stop!"

But Hank kept going. At the top of the stairs, we faced each other. Outside, someone screamed. Or was it me? Another scream. It *was* me. I shoved him. He grabbed me. I pushed him harder then lost my balance and fell. I was about to do a header down the stairs, but Hank grabbed me again, this time yanking me away from the stairs. I skidded across the floor. Hank tripped then turned. He reached for the banister but missed. His face flushed with surprise as he pitched backward. I could still hear his body hit each step. The thud, his grunts, his body finally landing.

24

Hank was paralyzed from the neck down. He's now home after two operations to stabilize his spine and months of extensive therapy at Legacy Rehabilitation Institute. His eyes still held the regret of his infidelity. We were both in our own way cut off at the neck.

While Hank was in therapy, I found text and email messages on his phone between Sophie and Hank that hadn't been on Sophie's phone or computer. He *had* broken it off. Sophie *had* threatened to tell me. Hank hadn't lied about that. He'd let her have access to his computer for redesigning the website. I could only guess he'd done that so she'd leave him alone. It hadn't work. Still, she begged him to take her back. She taunted him with having another lover. Just before flying to China, Hank wrote his final message. "Don't contact me again." Sophie wrote to him one more time and told him about the pregnancy. He answered with one word: "Vasectomy."

I was stunned. I had no idea he'd had a vasectomy. Not that it mattered. Neither of us wanted kids.

So Sophie *had* had another lover. Of course. I knew my

sister's M.O. How much had she kept from me? What had finally pushed her over the edge?

Not knowing was worse than knowing.

The reality, however, frightened me—I might never know. I had no place to turn to, no one to ask. Since Hank had returned home, he wouldn't utter her name.

25

Months passed. Between the specialists, the lawyers, the business, I ran at a frenzied speed. Hank's business affairs were frozen until the lawyers settled his share. Most of the equity in the house was used to pay for Hank's operations and therapy. Now he required full-time nursing care.

Carmen, Hank's nurse, lived at our house. I barely had enough to pay the monthly bills, never mind Carmen.

I'd filed a complaint against my ex-boss for sexual harassment. I had no money coming in and lots going out.

I sat with Hank in the evenings after meetings with medical people, researching possible reversals of his particular paralysis, and in my research, I found one.

He could have an operation that seemed viable, but he'd need to go outside the States. It cost fifty thousand dollars and had to happen fast before he deteriorated further. Financially, me flipping burgers wouldn't cut it. But I needed to know if this operation was legit.

How to verify the information and positive reviews? If Sophie were alive, I could have had her check the website and maybe determine its legitimacy. One of the clients I'd defended was an IT guy, not one of the sleaze bags, just a guy who got caught screwing with a company's internal communications after they'd busted his union and did away with benefit packages. He couldn't do what I needed because he was strictly monitored, so he turned me on to a hacker. I had to set up a SnapChat account, as that was the only way to contact her or him. The hacker's name was Snoop. I had to laugh.

Snoop confirmed the site's legitimacy and reviews. "and no bots," Snoop wrote.

I chuckled. And no caps in the messages either. I asked how to send payment for the info.

"thanks/no $/you defended IT pal."

We ended the session with me thinking Hank might be able to walk again.

But 50K? ASAP?

During the day, I begged for bank loans but was turned down. Our financial circumstances sucked. I thought of interviewing with small law firms, but I couldn't wait that long for the hiring process and paycheck.

Over-educated, overqualified, I'd painted myself into a corner, so I came up with a plan, disgusting as it was.

I didn't remember how I'd heard about Ashley Madison, a site where married men and women hooked up. Maybe defending criminals? If that was their way of cheating anonymously, it was my way of making fast chunks of cash. But I needed help in identifying the ones with money who I could blackmail.

I sent Snoop a message, explaining my plan to blackmail cheaters on Ashley Madison but I wanted to vet the guys I found. Could she find out if they fit a profile of "married with money?"

"yeah/no worries. combo internet searches&social engineering."

Whatever the hell that was.

"no charge/hate mutherfuckers who cheat."

Did that mean Snoop was female? Not necessarily. I liked her messages. Kind of like having poet e.e. cummings for a hacker. Plus, I understood what she wrote. No lingo that needed interpretation.

Snoop eliminated the cheats with a record for assault and with social media activity that raised alarms. She had a good nose for axing the needy, aggressive and weird.

When I joined Ashley Madison, I used a fake name and checked out some of the vetted leads. For four weeks, I secretly videoed the sexual encounters. The "date" had to pay 5K, or I'd send the video to his wife. Half the men paid. Half laughed in my face, even when I pointed a gun at them. But no one reported me. Showed how much they trusted the police or how honest they were.

I should have felt like shit about all this, but I was laser-focused on the 50K. If I needed further motivation, I'd think about Sophie and Hank. Whatever it took, I was reclaiming my husband and my marriage.

By the fifth week, I only had 10K to go. I was almost there. I made an online appointment for Hank's operation and received instructions for what that entailed. I waved the printed material in front of Hank. "You're going to walk again!" But his eyes didn't light up. I dropped to the floor and put my head in his lap. "You're going to walk. You will."

When I looked up, a tear ran down his face.

26

I t was my last weekend as a blackmailer. I'd always scheduled the dates away from Eugene, sometimes Seattle, sometimes Ashland, this time Portland.

As I arrived, the fog rolled up from the river, and a mercury-colored blanket enveloped the city. I navigated my leased Lexus along one-way, downtown streets until I pulled up to the Hotel Vintage at 4th and Broadway.

"Damn." I tugged at the red leather miniskirt that kept riding up my ass. Steve, my "date," had requested this outfit, something "mod," he'd said. I unfastened the seatbelt and buttoned my trench coat. I was forty-three and felt ridiculous wearing the miniskirt, knee-high boots, and gray schoolboy cap. The vintage shop, however, swore this look was back in style. Style? What did I know?

A light rain fell. A young doorman, charming and dutiful, opened the car door. "Welcome to the Hotel Vintage." His smile twinkled like polished silver. His eyes shone. I gave the young man a big smile, tapped into sexy, and handed him my key fob, overnight bag, and a tip. I wanted to lie down, a short rest, but couldn't. I would meet Steve in ninety minutes.

I caught my reflection in the hotel's window, once again not recognizing myself. As a criminal lawyer, I'd worn an expensive, fitted suit that served as armor. The adrenaline rush of trial work had kept me sharp and eager and exhausted in a good way. I loved performing before a judge or jury. Now there were dates instead of trials. My brunette hair was long and woven with different shades of blonde. I individualized my outfits for each victim. I flirted and charmed.

I hated it—all the men, sex, extortion. How dirty I felt. No matter how many times I showered, no matter how much I scrubbed and douched. No matter how many meds I took. I deserved never to feel clean. First I killed an innocent man. Now I demanded hush money from cheaters.

27

I nside Hotel Vintage's open lobby space—all bright blues and reds and polished wood—I welcomed the relief from the cold gray winter. I straightened my shoulders and headed to the bar.

My gut said this date, Steve, was a scumbag in some way. There were so many of them out there now. So many since the election. The whole world had gone berserk. I worried that Steve wouldn't like this place, though he'd picked it. I made all my dates pick the rendezvous spot. Steve told me he was wild about retro. Despite its name, Hotel Vintage was not retro.

I checked the gun nestled in my shoulder bag. I popped a med. Two drinks along with the med might get me through tonight. As I passed by a white leather couch, I noticed a pillow emblazoned with "I Try To Behave."

I said out loud, "That's a laugh."

I'd been talking to myself a lot lately.

At the bar, I took the nearest stool and ordered a Manhattan. The bartender asked if I'd like to try one of his signature cocktails instead.

"The bartenders in town have a contest every year to win best signature cocktail. But maybe you're a wine drinker?"

"Hell, no," I said. "Being in this hotel, I should be, but I like my liquor."

He whispered, "Me too, but don't tell the management."

We laughed. It felt good to laugh.

When my drink came, I sipped and nodded at the bartender in appreciation. I checked both my business and home cells. Nothing from Carmen, Hank's nurse. Good. No message from tonight's "date." Not good. What if he didn't show? What if he didn't pay the 5K after I threatened to show his wife the video? The ones who had refused so far said their wives didn't care if they were having affairs. I hoped Steve wasn't one of those. Or an undercover cop. So far I'd been lucky.

A message popped up from Sam, tomorrow's date. "Are we still on?"

I messaged back, "Yes. Tomorrow. Where and when?"

Sam seemed sweet but nervous. We'd talked on the phone. He was a newbie.

Tonight's guy, Steve, was a different story.

I pushed my empty glass toward the bartender. "Again?" he asked. I nodded.

Snoop's research had uncovered Steve's love of classic racing cars, trips to Monaco and Cannes, and baccarat. He must have thought he was James Bond. He used a fake profile on Ashley Madison, not mentioning any of his luxury habits. But maybe he didn't want to attract someone who wanted a fling with a rich guy. Made me suspicious though. Plus, he was the only date who had asked me to wear a costume.

While I waited for my second drink, I looked up the four-floor atrium, a dizzying sight of crazy geometric angles with one-half black and white and the other half gold and light. A split personality. Kind of like me. A circular staircase of wood and wrought iron reached the first floor. A modern, white grape-cluster chandelier hung over the lobby. Modern spiff. Classy.

Maybe I could take Steve for 10K instead of 5. Stabbing pains in my stomach again.

A drop-dead gorgeous guy stepped up to the bar and smiled at me. A woman joined him and took his arm. She was his equal in the looks department. She turned, met my eye, and said, "You're beautiful!"

I didn't know what to say. Was this a setup? Had Steve set up a swap or orgy? But then the man and woman joined another couple at the opposite end of the bar. I guzzled down my second drink, embarrassed.

I felt a tap on my shoulder and jumped.

"There's my bird. Let's look at you."

I turned.

Steve smiled. He had thick-lashed blue eyes, a thin Fu Manchu mustache, and a smile that lifted off like a rocket. But he was also crusty, his skin mottled and leathery from the elements. He appraised me. I returned the once-over.

Flashback to the Summer of Love. Steve wore a 60s rocker outfit down to the hip-hugging, striped, bell-bottom pants. His brown leather jacket had fringe, and he was skinny as a stick.

I suppressed a laugh. For some reason my gut said *Run*, but the money forced me to stay.

I stood. "Hello, Steve."

He took my hand, turned it over, and kissed my palm. Hmmm.

I slipped into vixen mode. "*Very* nice to meet you."

28

Steve opened the door to our hotel room. High ceiling, clean lines, neutral colors, modern art, and floor-to-ceiling curtains along the far wall windows. A bright red couch reminded me of seduction and blood. A small dining nook with a round table, a globe lamp hanging in the center, and four white leather and chrome chairs could have accommodated a poker game. The bed, all pale whites and cream with a blue as transparent as gin. I walked around the room, my nerves flaring, my stomach unsettled.

"Looks a little retro, don't you think?" I said.

Then the meds and alcohol kicked in, and the fuzzy cloak of not caring enveloped me.

Steve set my overnight bag near the far side of the bed, the one I always slept on at home, with the ease of someone who had done this many times. I wondered if Steve did this for the same reason that Hank did, that a man took the side closest to the door to protect against intruders.

"I've ordered champagne. Can I order anything else for you?" he asked.

Steve had an English accent? What? That hadn't come

up in Snoop's research. He had to be roleplaying. Just like the clothes.

He helped me remove my coat and whistled appreciatively. "Nice legs."

No one has ever told me I had nice legs. Never. It was all too ... too ... smarmy. Too ... cliché in some weird way. Plus, he looked way older than his photo. Maybe this was some unfulfilled dream he had for himself, to have been a rock-'n'roll star. But maybe it was his way of having fun. Like people who dressed up for comic con conventions.

"What can I do to make you comfortable?" he asked.

I wanted to say, *Send me back to the time before my sister's suicide, before finding out the truth about Hank, before Paris, before. ...*

I had a bad feeling, and it wasn't the roleplaying. Something wasn't right with this guy. I grabbed my coat. "Look, I'm sorry, but this isn't going to work."

He stepped back. "Have I done something wrong? Have I scared you?" His accent was still thick, and I couldn't understand why there was nothing in my research about him being English.

"I ... I don't know what it is, but it doesn't feel right. Something's off, and I have good instincts." I said this more for his benefit than mine. My instincts sucked.

I walked over to the bed for my overnight bag. There was a knock at the door. I grabbed my things and before I could make it to the door, a waiter wheeled in champagne and a tray of hors-d'oeuvres.

"I thought you might be hungry," Steve said.

Food. So Steve wasn't rushing it. Maybe I was wrong about him.

Steve tipped the waiter, and before I could make up my mind, the waiter was gone and I was left standing in the middle of the room with my bag and my coat over my arm.

Put your big girl panties on, I could hear my sister say.

I set the bag down. I was overreacting. I had to be.

Steve still stood in the middle of the room, a worried look on his aging face.

"I'm not comfortable with any of this," I repeated, this time in my courtroom voice, neutral, non-accusatory, factual. "I don't think you're English. I don't think your name is Steve. This act bothers me." I hesitated. "Plus, you've called all the shots and never asked if I wanted to play Patty Boyd bird, just given me instructions." He said nothing. I cleared my throat. "Am I right, about you not being English?"

"I'm surprised you know about Patty Boyd. You're young."

No English accent that time. No charm. He didn't like his cover blown.

"I don't feel young, and I'm not into this. I just want a nice romp with a married man so I can have what I don't have at home."

"That's what they all say."

"What?" I couldn't believe he'd just said that. He walked toward me. I stepped back.

"Oh, for God's sake, relax." In one swift movement, he grabbed the champagne and popped the cork. The *pop* made me jump. He poured a glass and downed it. He poured another and handed it to me. "Well, you sure spoiled this little fantasy of mine." He chuckled. With a relaxed slouch, he took a chair at the table and looked me over. "Go. Go ahead. Leave. The moment's spoiled, my one break from reality. I really thought you'd be fun. Serves me right for thinking."

I shook my head. "When did men get so petulant and self-centered?" I asked. He didn't respond. "I don't need your permission to leave." The champagne was good. I thought of putting down my purse, then thought again.

Seeing the 5-10K go up in smoke, I said, "Since we're not going to go through with this, let's tell the truth." I drank half the champagne. I needed a cigarette. "What's your real name? I know from online that you used an alias for Ashley Madison."

He raised his glass. "Really?"

I rolled my eyes. "Are you an out of work actor?"

"Don't insult me."

"Are you a gigolo?"

He laughed. "Are you *trying* to piss me off?"

"I bet you have money. You gamble at Cannes. You race. Why aren't you on the other dating site, the one for married people who are millionaires?"

"What? And date women who are wealthy?" He had a half smile that was unfortunately sexy. "Why would I do that? Besides, I don't want to hurt my wife. As we used to say in the 60s, she's a groovy chick."

I almost rolled my eyes. I didn't believe him.

He pointed to a chair. "Would you please sit? You might as well enjoy the champagne and hors-d'oeuvres. Keep me company for a while."

"Only if you order me Scotch."

"Don't like champagne?"

"This is good champagne, but no. It brings back bad memories."

He called room service and ordered a bottle of their best Scotch. At least he had taste—when he wasn't dressing like an old hippy.

"What's the matter?"

I collapsed into a chair and realized I'd been gripping the gun in my shoulder bag so hard my fingers had gone numb. "My hand's gone to sleep."

"Must be that gun you keep fondling. Are you a lawyer, a cop, or a PI?" he asked. "Samantha Spade, Undercover?"

I busted out laughing. "You're an asshole."

"I love a dirty mouth on a woman."

"Yeah, but your pickup lines suck."

"It happens."

I pushed the champagne glass across the table. "I was a lawyer. I recently took PI courses."

"Why?"

"Needed to."

"To investigate the men you date on Ashley Madison?" He chuckled. None of that seemed to bother him.

"Something like that."

"Now you're the one who needs new lines."

We both grinned.

"Look, why don't I get you another room for the night. On me." He popped an hors-d'oeuvre into his mouth. "Or you can go home to your husband and get him to fuck you since *this* isn't happening."

"He can't. He's in a wheelchair."

Steve shook his head and ate another cracker. "I've heard that one before, too."

Yeah, Steve was a dick.

Before room service delivered the bottle, Steve grabbed a glass from the minibar, filled it with ice, twisted off the tops of two small whiskeys, poured both dramatically into the glass, and handed it to me. I greedily slugged down half. The warmth moved from pelvis to face. Steve watched me like I was some kind of science project.

"We argued," I finally said. "I tripped at the top of the

stairs. Would have gone down, but he yanked me back. He lost his balance and did a header."

"Shit."

I nodded, polished off the rest of my drink, and to my horror, started crying.

Then I burped.

We both laughed. I dabbed my wet cheeks. "Sorry about that."

The bottle of Scotch arrived. He tried to get me to talk more, but I wouldn't. Even though I was tipsy from the two bar cocktails, the champagne, the scotch and the med, I didn't divulge that I had planned to blackmail him.

"You should know," he said, "that the other profile of me, the one that sounds like James Bond, is a crock too. I'm nothing like that. I put that up as a joke, but also to see if any of the dates did any research on me. How about you?"

Surprised with this admission, I blurted out, "I killed someone."

Silence.

Then he raised his glass and said, "You're quite a dame." He drank. "I suppose you're an assassin."

He didn't believe me. I knew he wouldn't. Who would? But why had I said that?

In the morning when I woke, he was gone. I jumped out of bed. A wicked pain stabbed between the eyes. I checked my shoulder bag. The gun and purse were still there. I stumbled over to the coffee maker but couldn't deal with it. In the bathroom, I hated what I saw in the round, lit mirror. The crying last night had laid waste to my eye makeup. Then there had been the long, interminable attempt at screwing, two drunks pretending they could, but couldn't. Pitiful. I called room service for coffee, walked to the window, and looked down on an alley. When I sat on the red couch, I discovered five one hundred dollar bills splayed out like a fan. No note. No explanation. Now I was nothing but a mid-price hooker who hadn't delivered the goods.

I wanted to rip the bills into tiny little pieces but slipped them into my purse instead.

29

A sudden cold downpour forced me into a run on SW Washington. I dove into Blue Star Donuts. It was crowded. Someone accidentally elbowed me. The smell of fried dough made my nostrils quiver. I got in line. Columbia raincoats and steamy bodies.

Steve's scent—fir and fungi with a tinge of cigar—lingered, even after a long shower and excess scrubbing. The conversations in the bakery blended and blurred as if I were under water. I distracted myself by studying the donut case. My mouth watered. I ordered three brioche donuts—blueberry bourbon basil, chocolate almond ganache, and an old-fashioned—plus a large cup of coffee. I forked over a twenty. The donuts were expensive but worth it. As the sign said, these were donuts for adults. My current job—seducing and blackmailing strangers for money—was definitely "adult." But I was pissed at Steve.

I squeezed in at the counter along the window. Standing-room-only. On my left a young couple fed each other cream-filled donuts, laughing as they made a mess. I wanted to laugh like that again. Next to me, a man in a suit read the

Wall Street Journal. The lingering smell of pot stuck to him. Everywhere I went now, that sweet skunky stink wafted up in the oddest places.

My headache had finally dialed down to a hum. I ate one donut and sipped the coffee. I'd developed another bad habit, besides the cigarettes and affairs. Now after each date, I found a donut or pastry shop. I heard that overeating stemmed from unresolved emotional issues, but I knew exactly where this one had come from—killing Gerard. The morning after, I'd eaten all four Parisian pastries I'd bought the day before—the pain au chocolate, the éclair, a cream puff and a lemon tart. The guilt of killing someone should have plastered on the pounds. I should be obese. Instead, I stayed as skinny as Kate Moss. Hank wouldn't have approved. He liked a little flesh on his woman. Now it didn't matter. We were both skeletons of our former selves.

I watched a woman across from me—shoulder length straight hair; a tasteful outfit; perfectly applied makeup— and realized I was looking at my reflection in the window. I was startled. Sophie had told me I would be attractive if I changed my hair and ditched the suits.

I ate the second donut. The man next to me rustled his paper. I missed the morning paper with Hank. We used to wake before dawn, share coffee and newspapers, talk politics and business.

Who was I kidding? The days of sharing newspapers had lasted maybe a year. With my first position at a big law firm, I'd begun skipping the morning ritual to work on case notes instead. Hank's engineering company had grown so quickly he was often out of the country.

A couple in line argued. Their voices rose. The man grabbed her arm, but the woman wrenched away. When the clerk interrupted, they turned to him as if nothing had happened.

I stuffed a large bite of the third donut into my mouth. Hard driving rain smacked against the window, reminding me of the day Hank came home from China, our fight, him falling down the stairs.

A coffee thermos hit the floor and made a loud metallic ring. I jumped.

The man with the newspaper said, "Sorry 'bout that," as he bent to pick up his thermos.

Shaky and hungover, I brushed crumbs from the counter and headed to the door where a sign read, "Stay calm. Eat donuts."

Outside on Washington, I pulled up my coat's collar and headed toward Pioneer Square. The rain had stopped. A heavy mist enveloped me.

30

Under an awning, I leaned a shoulder against a brick wall and stared into a store of bright boho furniture. Ah, to be somewhere sunny, somewhere exotic, with no memory of my past.

My phone dinged. A text. From Steve.

"How about a repeat? Haven't been able to stop thinking about you."

Jesus.

My stomach clenched. Why would he even want a repeat? I deleted the message and hurried along the sidewalk.

Five blocks later, past Pioneer Square and near the Portland Art Museum, the mist turned to rain again. I opened my umbrella, but a sudden gust of wind whipped it from my hand and out to the street. I bolted after it. A car skidded and honked. My chest pounded as I chased the umbrella into the park blocks. The homeless clustered under the trees, some in raincoats, others wrapped in blue plastic tarps or plastic bags. When I finally grabbed the umbrella, I almost fell over a pile of dirty blankets that moved. A woman's ravaged face peeked out. I peered into her eyes and saw a life that could have been mine. I shuddered.

The woman didn't beg for help. She was probably past caring. I had once given a woman with a dog and a child a twenty-dollar bill, and half an hour later caught her in Albertson's buying lottery tickets. I hesitated, then handed this woman my umbrella and slipped her one of the hundred dollar bills that Steve had left last night on the coffee table. Wouldn't Steve have hated that? I thought so.

The woman didn't say thank you or god bless. Instead, tears filled her rheumy eyes, and she quickly hid the money in her clothes.

"Get something to eat," I said, thinking how pathetic that sounded.

I was close to tears as I rushed off to the Museum. Had I done the right thing? Would it put the woman in danger?

I once would have called Sophie and told her about this encounter. Now I had no one call.

31

At the flat, brick building of the Portland Art Museum, I shook myself like a dog and walked up the steps to the three entries of glass, steel, and engraved marble. I wondered if Hank remembered our honeymoon visit here. We'd rented audio sets for an exhibit of 17th-century Dutch painters. He soaked up details. "Did you know the long, white clay smoking pipes are called Gouda?"

"Like the cheese?" I'd said jokingly.

During the audio section on Dutch women, he pulled me close and whispered over the earpiece. "I bet you love this." I did. Dutch women—unlike other 17th century European women—could engage in business and sign contracts.

Hank said, "We'd all be better off if women ran the world." At least Hank didn't have to deal with where the world was headed now.

At the top of the stairs, for the first time, it hit me hard. I really missed him. The conversations, the ease, the intimacy. I raised my face skyward, the rain blending with my tears. I was lonely. I'd fallen in love with my husband all over again.

Oh, how I loathed my sister for not only taking her own life but mine. I didn't want to hate Sophie, but I'd killed an innocent man because of her. And I'd lost my husband.

I deep-sixed my feelings. I couldn't hate my sister. I couldn't. Whatever had hurt my sister, hurt her so much she'd hung herself. I needed to remember that. Somehow, someday, I would find out what caused her suicide. Right now, however, it was all about paying for Hank's operation. Getting my Hank back.

I wiped my face and entered the Portland Art Museum where I paid the museum's entry fee, grabbed the current exhibit pamphlet, and rented a headset to plug into my phone.

On the first floor, I walked past exhibits without seeing. I climbed stairs with no thought of where I was going. On the second floor in the first room, while trying to find the audio on the museum's website, I glanced up and froze. A man, his back to me, stood before a large painting. He had a full head of dark brown hair, stocky build, he ... he. ... The shoes, the jeans, the brown bomber jacket, the. ... I walked toward him and reached out. "Hank?"

He turned and smiled. "I'm sorry," he said. "I'm afraid you've mistaken me for someone else."

I stepped backward then raced away. My feet felt spongy as I took the stairs to the third floor where I made my way to a corner window. The light hurt my eyes, my chest ached, and I just wanted to be home, snuggling with Hank, even though he couldn't embrace me. The city's sharp angles poked and prodded the gray blanket of my mind. I was like my sister's urn—a pretty vessel holding nothing but remains.

I breathed deep and long and desperate. All this reminiscing hurt and distracted.

"Buck up. Get your shit together." I pulled my body upwards like I was stretching canvas on a frame. Now was not the time to collapse. I had work to do.

My phone dinged with a text. "How about it? Want to finish what we started last night?"

Steve? Again?

I deleted the message. It was my own damn fault for having sex with him. Or trying to. I should have left early. But my gut had become as untrustworthy as a repeat offender.

I needed to get out of here.

Going down the stairs, I realized I was lost. I ducked into a lady's room where I squeezed into a stall and sat on the commode. I hugged myself, rocking back and forth. The smell of cleaning fluids, perfume, and old canvas filled my lungs. After wiping my nose, I pulled the silver pillbox from my shoulder bag and popped a med.

When I had the money for Hank's operation, I could stop "dating" and concentrate on what had pushed Sophie to suicide. My gut feeling said it hadn't been Hank turning her down, or Sophie's desire to steal him away. From my years in criminal law, I sensed something else was at work.

32

Outside the museum, the rain had stopped. Cars passed by, rubber hissed on wet pavement. City sounds intensified. I pulled up my coat collar, inhaled the moist air, and forced myself to walk.

A hangover headache, long overdue, clamped itself on my temples. The sky darkened. I regretted not buying an umbrella. Above me, thousands of crows landed in the park's bare-branched trees. They kept coming. They didn't dive. They didn't caw. The silence was eerie.

"What the hell does this mean?"

An older woman walking toward me said, "Are you all right, honey?"

"Just wondering about the crows," I said, pointing.

The woman glanced up. "Oh, that," she said as if she saw it every day.

I kept walking, but I couldn't feel my feet on the pavement and wondered if I was losing it. I ducked into South-park, an oyster bar and seafood restaurant. I wasn't hungry, but I needed to eat, needed something more substantial than donuts and coffee.

At the bar, I took a stool. I ordered a gin and tonic, and the Normandy Seafood Stew, something warm, something comforting, something that would vanquish my headache and numbness. I found no message from tonight's date. Damn. He should have sent me time and place.

My date, Sam, being a little neurotic, could have backed out. On the phone a few days earlier, I'd tried to reassure him that everything was fine, not to stress, that I'd done this before, and all my dates had been wonderful. That was a mistake. Desperate to keep him on the hook, I had divulged that my husband was paralyzed from the neck down. "Oh, I'm so sorry," he said, accepting this as fact, immediately empathizing and trusting me. I'd found that odd, but refreshing.

When the stew came, I took a small bite. It was delicious, but my stomach reacted. I waited. The bartender watched me. I hadn't touched my drink. Another bite of stew. The bartender asked if everything was OK. "I waited too long to eat," I said. He nodded as if he understood.

After managing to get down enough bites of the stew to activate my brain, I sipped my G&T and felt the first flush of energy. I had to start eating better and regularly. It was affecting my performance.

My cell dinged. A message from Snoop.

Sam or Samuel was one of the few men she'd been able to track via his wife's newsworthy philanthropy. Snoop had given him five stars.

"more info: he lost family fortune in Madoff-style ripoff/married into his social sphere/not hurting now."

I, however, was leery of Sam's sweet innocence. I had one of those before. The date had seemed innocent, even shy, but when it came to sex, he held me down and talked sick and nasty. I couldn't get out from under him fast enough.

After, I threw up and took a long shower with gardenia soap, anything to wash away his smell.

I checked my personal phone. Nothing from home.

I ate more stew, feeling much better, then drained my G&T. After paying the bill, I messaged Sam. "Are we still on for tonight?"

No response. Now what?

I was tempted to head home. Outside, the sidewalks were unusually quiet. I headed to the Hotel Vintage where my car was still parked, and near Pioneer Square, the smell of coffee drew my attention.

I was about to cross the street to Starbucks when I saw Conrad, the asshole from my old law firm who fired, then reported, me. What a piece of work. One time he'd put his hand between my legs in the elevator. I smacked his face. I was pretty sure that's what got me dismissed.

Ducking from view, I joined a group of people.

"Hey! Ang!" he yelled.

Shit, he saw me. As if I'd talk to him.

"Ang!" he shouted. "Hey, it's me, Conrad."

I kept walking as if he didn't exist.

33

At Hotel Vintage, I called for my car and waited in the lobby. The weekend was going sideways.

"Don't go paranoid," I said under my breath. But seeing Conrad here in Portland was like finding a rattler in your bathtub.

Plus, I didn't like coincidences or—as Sophie used to call them—"synchronistic occurrences." While I waited for my car, I tried to reason with myself. Conrad had a client in Portland. He was here to meet a possible new addition to the firm. He was working as a consultant to—

My phone dinged. Another message from Steve. What was his problem? I glanced around the lobby, wondering if he skulked nearby. I deleted the text and rushed outside.

"Can you get my car right away? I really need to leave."

The valet smiled. "Of course."

Another text. I almost deleted it before I saw it was from Sam.

"Yes. Still on. Looking forward to the evening."

My car came.

Another text.

"I would like to take you out to dinner. I made an eight o'clock reservation at St. Jack. I hope you like French food."

I hated anything French.

The valet held open the car door. As I slid in, I remembered Gerard. Gerard's kiss. What I'd done. I dug my nails into my palms to press the guilt into physical pain. When I stopped remembering, I wiped my hands on a napkin and struggled with the seat belt.

Another text.

"We have a room at Hotel deLuxe. You can go there anytime to settle in and freshen up. Their Rolls Royce will take you to the restaurant and me."

What the hell? Hank and I had honeymooned at the deLuxe, back when it was the Hotel Mallory.

"I can't do this."

The valet said, "What, Ma'am?"

"Nothing. Thank you."

He closed the door.

I drove off before realizing I'd forgotten to tip him.

I didn't know where I was.

First Steve. Then Conrad. Now this. I pulled over into an empty parking space.

Leaning back on the headrest, I peered through the moon-roof. Dark clouds hid the sun. I cracked my window. The smell of fried foods, gumbo and spices hit my nose. A pod of food carts covered a block of downtown between 9th and 10th. I was driving away from the river so I had to be on Washington. OK. I was going in the right direction.

I sat up.

Another text. I was afraid to look.

But it was Sam. "Everything all right?"

I messaged back, "Yes. Looking forward." Agreeing to dinner was a mistake.

I pulled down the visor and checked myself in the mirror. My mascara had run, and deep lines etched my mouth. I wetted another napkin with my tongue and rubbed away the mascara, causing red splotches under my eyes.

Time to regroup. The hotel was only a few blocks away. How had my life failed so miserably? I'd lost my sister, my job, my husband. Everyone and everything I loved. Now I was reduced to this? I broke the law instead of upholding the law. Yet I could argue legal interpretations all day, and night—except for killing Gerard.

When would karma catch up with me? What was I talking about? I didn't believe in karma. That had been a Sophie thing.

I rolled down all the windows and lit a cigarette, inhaling the soothing smoke mingled with the fogginess of a city that had once given me so much happiness.

34

Hotel deLuxe sat at the corner of 15th Avenue and Morrison. At four o'clock, I was already beat.

The traffic clogged intersections. Horns honked. Sirens went off in the distance. I could hear the congestion on the nearby freeway. There would be accidents in this weather, the oil-slick roads, the layer of rain, the hard grind of a work day, and road rage.

Once I'd been part of the grind. I guess I still was.

As I turned onto 15th, someone laid on a horn. I almost sideswiped a car. At the hotel entrance, I slammed on the brakes. My shoulder bag flew to the floor. I put the car in park and sat back.

A valet opened my door. "Welcome to the Hotel deLuxe."

I handed him my key fob, but I was shaking, and it dropped onto the concrete. The valet scooped it up.

I pulled myself together. "I have an overnight and dress bag in the trunk." Up ahead, the Rolls was parked along the curb.

The valet noticed where I was looking. "That's the hotel's vintage 1966 Rolls Royce Silver Cloud III Touring limo."

"Nice," I said as I tipped him. He handed me bag receipts.

Before I headed to the lobby, a turquoise Thunderbird slowly passed by the hotel. The driver looked directly at me. It was Steve. Shit.

The car sped up and turned the corner. The son-of-a-bitch *was* stalking me. I'd guessed he was a creep.

I hurried inside.

Happily, the hotel distracted me. Nothing reminded me of the old Mallory. Not the chandelier-lit marble-lined stairway. Not the lobby's gold Deco furnishings, white accents, and black details. A wall-high monitor that flashed movie stills of famous actors and actresses from the Hollywood Golden Age stopped me. The floor-to-ceiling screen showed a movie still of Marilyn Monroe, and I was reminded of Paris. The Metro advertisements, Marilyn on the floor in a negligee, reading a book. New Years. Gerard.

What had ever possessed me? How could I have done it? I wasn't violent. Yet I'd poisoned him and watched him die in front of me. Maybe if I'd had to use a gun or if I'd had to plunge a knife into his heart, I would never have killed him.

I couldn't breathe. I tried, but I couldn't suck down enough air. The room wobbled. I grabbed a post and worked my way to a chair.

This was what happened when I thought of Gerard. It was like being strangled with my own guilt. I pressed fingers hard against my closed eyes.

The moment passed. I forced my legs to stand. Steady. OK. I filled my lungs with air then walked to the front desk.

The woman at the desk took my name, another alias, Claire Kingsley. The woman smiled as if she knew the reason for the rendezvous. "Your husband said you were driving separately. He checked you into the Marlene Dietrich Suite." She held out the key card.

In the elevator, I leaned against the wall and cursed my sister. Had Sophie ever thought about what her suicide would do to *me*? Had she ever? Once? I'd killed an innocent man because of her.

Stop.

Stop now.

You made a mistake.

Think of Hank. What you were doing on your honeymoon. I shifted my bag to my other shoulder. Maybe it was good that I was here, at this hotel, to remind me of good times. Eating seafood at Jake's. Drinking cocktails at an outdoor table. Making love all night on the Mallory's famous round bed. Being happy, in love, not screwing for money.

The door opened on the seventh floor. A hall mirror discretely lit up with the name of the floor's director theme, "The Exiles." Perfect. At the end of the hall, I opened the door to room 721. Thankfully, I'd be able to relax for an hour or two.

I stepped in and gasped. The round bed.

The fucking universe was messing with me.

I dropped my shoulder bag and approached the bed like a dog sneaking up on a stranger.

On the bed were two delicate chocolates in a box. I threw the box across the room then laughed. This was like being pranked by a best friend—if I had a best friend.

I tore off my coat. Wait. I didn't remember this room. Had it been a corner suite? I didn't recall vibrant marigold-colored walls back then. Or apple-green floor-to-ceiling curtains.

Plus this bed was all white and cream. I didn't remember what it had for a bedspread when Hank and I were here, but I *did* remember having a hard time sleeping, even after all the lovemaking. Hank and I clung to each other. A bed with no ninety-degree angles felt dangerous as if we were explorers who set out on a voyage, thinking the earth was flat, and we'd fall off. We almost did a few times.

I hugged myself. Life had been so simple then. Falling off a bed a danger? Bring it on!

When I sat on the bed, I remembered how much we'd laughed. Hank carried me over the threshold, me yelling, "You'll hurt yourself!" He dropped me on the bed where we bounced up and down like little kids. Life was ahead of us. Even with the pressure of Hank launching his business and me having to pay back university loans while scrambling to find a position at a law firm, we loved our life.

That was why I take money from men who will never miss it. That is why I lie down for them, internally humiliated. I wanted Hank to walk again. I wanted my marriage back.

A loud knock at the door startled me. I sat frozen until I heard the porter call out, "I have your bags, ma'am." What was I so scared of? I let him in, he put my bags by the bed, and I tipped him. He left. Even with taking my meds, my nerves were fired up.

I walked to the window and turned. The room grew more familiar. I pictured Hank on the couch, his feet on the coffee table. Our first night. I had a surprise for him.

He'd asked, "Are we really going to the ballet tonight?"

"No. I'm blindfolding you and taking you down into an underground tunnel."

He stopped. "Really?" I loved that he'd looked a little horrified and excited.

In a sexy, breathy voice, I said, "B movies have always been my inspiration."

That night, when the taxi dropped us at the Ringside, Portland's most iconic steakhouse, Hank kissed me hard on the lips and said, "What a broad." I guessed beforehand what he'd order—prime rib, baked potatoes and the famous onion rings. The waiter, Bradford—God, I still remembered his name—could have been a stand-in for Robert Mitchum in *Angel Face*. Hank ordered a beer. I ordered a martini. During dessert, I handed him tickets, not for the ballet, but for *Spamalot* at the Keller Auditorium. He loved that crazy musical.

He'd grinned, shook his head, and said, "You little vixen."

A week after the honeymoon, Sophie and I were curled up on her couch in our PJs, smoking a joint, and I laughed as I told her about how I'd surprised Hank.

Sophie said, "Monty Python isn't very sexy."

"It's not always about sex, Sophie," I'd said.

Sophie snorted. "On your honeymoon it should be."

I quit telling her about the honeymoon—or anything else personal about Hank and me.

Every relationship Sophie had had, she'd mistaken physical attraction for love and never learned the difference. But there was something else—Sophie always thought she was saving the man, presenting herself as rescuing the husband from either an abusive or negligent wife. I'd fallen for her justifications. I'd wanted to believe her. But after a while. ...

"She enjoyed the conquest," I said aloud as if delivering a closing argument before a jury.

I guzzled a bottle of complimentary water while considering a selection of adult items—prophylactics, massage oil, a "Seduction Kit."

Had Sam been here before? Was this whole innocent act just that, an act? If Snoop was right and Sam's wife was a Lesbian, I understood the need to date. But why marry in the first place?

Something was wrong with this date, too.

I grabbed both my bags and my shoulder bag, ready to flee.

"Pull yourself together," I shouted. I dropped my bags.

Whatever happened to the woman who could handle anything thrown her way?

Time to regroup. I hung the "Quiet on the Set" sign on the doorknob, poured a minibar bottle of scotch into a glass, and slugged it down.

Sam would pay 10K tonight. I'd get through the sex. Hell, I should be able to outdo a Lesbian wife.

After, when I was home, I'd push the lawyers to settle Hank's business. They'd taken too damn long. Hank had developed eighty percent of their patents. He deserved better than this—and the partners knew it.

35

For a moment I had no idea where I was. I sat up abruptly, wiped the drool from the side of my mouth, and remembered. My cell showed I'd slept for an hour, something I never did.

In the bathroom, the mirror reflected a face I didn't recognize. This life was killing me. My cell rang.

"Hi, Claire? This is Sam. Do you like the room?"

Sam? Who was Sam? Sam ... oh, right. Yes. Him.

Wait. How had he known I was here?

As if he'd read my mind, he said, "I called the hotel to see if you'd checked in. Is there anything you need? The Rolls will bring you to the restaurant. Go down to the lobby at seven-forty-five. Is that OK? Claire?"

Was this guy a control freak or was he really just trying to be nice? I didn't deserve it. I didn't want it. I reached for a cigarette and remembered I couldn't smoke in the room. I headed over to the minibar.

"I'm fine, Sam. Just fine."

"Um, I ... I ..."

I poured another scotch, no ice. "What, Sam?"

"I just want this to be perfect."

Perfect? That was the kiss of death. "Are you sure you want to do this?"

Silence.

Stupid. Stupid to have asked. I slugged back the scotch and dropped into the soothing role I'd had to take with him. "Look, I'm sure it *will* be perfect, Sam. We'll have a lovely dinner, come back to the room and chill, get to know each other a little more, and then ... we'll snuggle a little, warm up to each other before we do anything. Sound good?"

More silence.

"Sam?"

Oh god. was he crying? Or laughing?

"Thank you, Claire." He snuffled. "You don't know how much that means."

I sighed. He was crying. I felt for the guy. "OK, see you at eight. And thanks for the Rolls."

"My pleasure," he said, this time with enthusiasm.

After I hung up, I finished the scotch and hugged myself. Jeez, this guy didn't want a quick fuck. He wanted to be in love. I couldn't help feeling a tug at my heart.

I was such an asshole. But I couldn't go soft now. Even if he really *was* a nice guy. Maybe I could give him what he wanted, a real date, a romantic evening, like a high price hooker. My gut said Sam was playing it straight, and he really needed romance, even if it was fake and cost him. Maybe his wife being a Lesbian had given him permission to date as long as it was discrete. Maybe it was an arrangement.

Wait. If it was an arrangement, he wouldn't care if his wife saw the video. He wouldn't pay the money—unless the wife wanted to protect the perception of a real marriage. That was probably what this was about—Sam helping her keep the perception of being a happily-married hetero woman. He *had* to sneak around.

The scotch loosened my limbs, and my face muscles relaxed. I walked the room, hoping I could hold it together tonight. I was stuck on this mystery about Sam and why he'd been forced to use Ashley Madison instead of meeting women the usual way, whatever that was. Even if the wife paid him to act as a husband because she needed the cover, why would a romantic like Sam lower himself to use Ashley Madison, the antithesis of romance sites.

Come to think of it, how had *I* found out about the site?

It took a moment before I remembered.

Sophie.

Sophie had heard about Ashley Madison when the news reported someone had hacked their website. Like so many things celebrity, the story had captivated Sophie who called me with the latest. "All these rich celebrities and politicians used it and have been outed. Why didn't they just buy a hooker?"

I hadn't paid much attention. At the time, the law firm's founder, Conrad's father, had dangled the possibility of a partnership. I had the money to buy in. I'd worked hard, so hard I almost ended up in the hospital. But Conrad's father died of heart attack a week later, and I knew I was no favorite of Conrad who took over the firm.

Sophie's interest in the "dating" site became an obsession. Her obsessiveness drove me to research Ashley Madison. I found other sites that provided the same type of service, including the private one for millionaires. Had Sophie dabbled on any of these sites? She wasn't married, but how would they have known? Sophie swore she never used dating sites, but that could have been a lie too. Part of my sister's secret life. She *had* erased the history on her computer.

I walked faster, now feeling caged in this room. I'd never known Sophie, not really. It was as if the sweet and adoring sister I'd known was nothing more than my own creation. The Sophie I'd known was gone. My brilliant husband was a silent, inert partner. I wasn't even me anymore.

"If I'm not me, who am I?"

Hearing a voice made me jump. My voice.

I held my hands over my ears and breathed with ferocity. So what if I'd blackmailed these men? These men cheated. 5K was a pittance to them. They weren't innocent. I was doing it to save Hank who deserved to be saved. I was doing it for *Hank,* damn it!

I grabbed my overnight bag. Yes, I might have been doing this for Hank, but that didn't mean I had to be a Sophie look alike or a man magnet. I could resurrect the Ang who'd fallen in love with Hank, the man who loved and appreciated me as I was.

That did it. No more sexy outfits. No more Kardashian makeup. I threw on slacks, a blouse and flats, ran a comb through my hair, pinched my cheeks, and added lip gloss. Relief. I wanted to feel classy again. I wanted to be in control again.

I began by prepping the room for my night with Sam. From my bag, I pulled out a tiny video camera disguised as a digital clock and exchanged it for the one next to the bed. I adjusted the video focus, tested the angle, and set the timer. It could be changed later if need be.

Surprisingly, dressed again like this reminded me of the woman I used to be. I told myself that justice was blind. I would stay away from the truth, from what I'd done, and head toward the future. One more night doing this. Only one more. Then I was free. Hank would walk. I would never pay for my mistake in killing Gerard, but I could help another man live again.

But as hard as I tried, the room closed in on me again. So I grabbed my laptop and headed to the Driftwood Room for a martini and breathing space.

I took a seat at the bar. The menu of signature cocktails and clever names—Rio Bravo, Sideburn, Ginger Rogers— took too much concentration, so I ordered a dirty martini and opened my laptop. By the time my drink came, I'd written an emphatic email to Hank's business lawyers, encouraging them to step it up. I inserted that if it took much longer, I'd have to resort to hiring my own lawyer to protect my interests, something I should have done from the start since I was Hank's beneficiary. For them to understand, I added how difficult it was to keep up with Hank's hefty caregiving and medical bills.

Then I hit send.

I was about to check Ashley Madison and Snoop, but a male voice whispered in my ear, "I like what you've done with your hair." I turned.

Conrad. Jesus!

"How come you didn't answer me when I called your name?"

He stood too close. He reeked of cologne. The firm's secretarial staff had complained that if he hugged you—and he liked hugging among other things—they'd smell like him all day. Like imprinting his prey. No one ever wanted to get in an elevator with him—for numerous reasons. If there was one person who deserved to be fired, it was Conrad. But he owned the firm now.

I closed my laptop, slid off the stool on the opposite side, and left a twenty on the bar. The gun in my purse gave me a satisfied feeling when I thought of using it on this piece of shit. Instead, I looked him in the eye and said nothing.

Before I escaped, two men in suits appeared. They greeted Conrad. I stepped around them. Out in the lobby, I found a chair hidden from sight of the bar entrance.

No man had made me as angry as Conrad. He held power over everyone who was either beneath or beholden to him. When Conrad fired me, he accused me of giving evidence to opposing council, evidence that convicted our client. I did do it because I couldn't stomach a rapist getting off, especially a rich, powerful one who had been up on rape charges before, and a good friend of Conrad's. I suspected they had shared many stories of conquest.

I was sure my firing had more to do with my refusal of Conrad's sexual advances. I'd known others at the firm who had operated outside legal boundaries, and they'd been reprimanded, not fired. In fact, the way Conrad had operated, I had worried at some point that we'd all end up in jail for his illegal maneuvers. Even though danger was a criminal lawyer's constant companion—the vengeful girlfriend of an incarcerated boyfriend; threats from a dirty cop; slashed tires—you needed everyone in the firm to have your back. I hadn't trusted this prick because of the immorality that he'd brought to the firm.

"Conrad's probably a lousy lay," I said under my breath as I hid in this cloistered corner of the lobby and tried to regain my composure. "Probably doesn't know the first thing about satisfying a woman."

But hell, few of my dates had either. Sometimes, if the guy seemed decent, I'd ask him out of curiosity why he was screwing around on his wife. Each guy had given me a version of "I love my wife, but she doesn't like sex."

Ironically most of my dates knew nothing about satisfying a woman. Hank did. He'd also taken direction well.

I stood, still shaky, and checked the time. It was too late for a shower. I sneaked a peek toward the bar, hoping to walk past to the elevator without being seen.

But Conrad and the two men stood in the entrance, shaking hands and nodding.

And with them ... was Steve

I dropped back against the wall, out of sight. My mind mixed thick and muddy like leftover wall paints. Nothing made sense. Why would Steve be talking to Conrad?

After they left, I stood on wobbly legs and tried to tell myself it had nothing to do with me. Why would it? Steve was some kind of consultant. Conrad was a lawyer. This had to be some kind of business meeting. That would explain why I'd seen Steve drive by the hotel earlier. But something gnawed at me with tiny sharp teeth, leaving my insides raw.

I rushed to the elevator to leave my laptop in the room and hoped the men were gone when I caught the Rolls to the restaurant. Sam now felt like an island far away from a continent of paranoia.

36

The Rolls Royce dropped me at St. Jack almost half an hour early. Before this area had been dubbed the Trendy-Third of Portland, Hank and I used to enjoy an egg cream and pastrami Reuben at Kornblatt's.

I walked up the street, away from NW 23rd, and lit up. The cigarette trembled in my hand. By the time I'd walked around the block, and people had glared at me for smoking, I was back at the restaurant ten minutes early.

At eight o'clock, Sam arrived, and the host seated us. Sam was tall with a runner's build. From his profile page, I hadn't been able to tell. I remembered his photo, a combination of kind mouth and eyes. We'd had a lawyer at the firm with eyes like that. She could get any truth out of a client. Sam, like that lawyer, exuded empathy. I thought. But then, given Sophie, Hank and Gerard, I was not the best judge of character.

Under his jacket, he wore a black t-shirt with a scarab design. After we took our seats, I noticed his long nose and a twist to his mouth. I couldn't quite explain it, but it gave me a moment's pause. The twist disappeared as he smiled.

He extended his hand. "I'm so happy to meet you, Claire."

He set a leather bag on the floor. From our phone calls, I thought he'd be awkward and gawky. Instead, he sat with poise and grace. He took up space like a world-class chef in a modern kitchen.

"Have you been here before?" he asked.

"No. But I've heard great things about it." I hadn't, but it was something to say.

"I still haven't figured out why they don't call this place the French version, *St. Jacques*. Maybe they knew everyone would say *Jack*, so they decided to play along." He laughed at himself and shrugged. "Would you like to start with wine? Or a cocktail?" He pulled a napkin across his lap, all the while keeping eye contact with me. "I remember your profile said you weren't a wine drinker." He grinned. "I thought that might be a strategy to eliminate certain men who had to show off their sommelier-like knowledge as a prelude to sex?"

I grinned back. OK. Sam had a sense of humor. "Something like that," I said.

We studied the *boissons* menu.

"What do you say we try the French Pearl 12?"

I found it on the menu: Tanqueray gin, Pernod Absinthe, lime, mint. I wasn't sure, never having absinthe before. But I couldn't concentrate on the other drinks. "Yes, that's fine." I leaned back. "Would you have ordered wine if I had?" This sounded snarky, but I'd decided to be direct from now on. Be myself. Besides, I really wanted to know.

"I'm not a wine connoisseur. My wife is. She insists it's an art." Now he showed an edge of uncertainty as he had on the phone. "Do you mind if I mention my wife?"

Sam was either real smooth or a no bullshitter. At least

he had the decency to ask about mentioning his wife. "No. I don't mind as long as it's in context. And as long as you don't mind me *not* talking about my husband."

After the drinks arrived, I let him order the hors-d'oeuvres. After he ordered seared foie gras, we talked about the political situation.

"It's a relief," he said, "to talk with someone who's also outraged at what's happening." He raised his glass to me. I relaxed a little.

"So you can't talk to your wife about politics?"

He didn't answer. Instead, he told me about a nonprofit he had founded, a veterinarian clinic that served animals of the homeless. I was impressed.

For dinner I ordered Duck à la Cerise, Gerard Mussels Marinière.

Our conversation continued, eclectic and relaxed. I told him as little as possible about me. He was generous to a fault. We seemed to have a lot in common. That's why I didn't have dinner with my dates. Blackmail was tough when you liked a person. From his leather bag, Sam pulled out a small gift bag and handed it to me. "For you," he said.

I sat back.

"I wanted to give you something for being so kind to me on the phone. You made me feel very comfortable doing this. Thank you."

"I don't accept gifts."

"Please," Sam said.

Out of curiosity, I unwrapped what felt like a small box, but turned out to be a wooden frame that enclosed glass on each side and displayed a two-inch beetle mounted on a pin. The beetle's colors flashed green and neon blue. I didn't have a fear of bugs and examined the beetle. "Is this real? The colors are ... are—"

"It's a Phalacrognathus muelleri. Commonly known as a Rainbow Stag Beetle. It's found in the rainforests of Queensland, Australia."

When I was a kid, I'd bring home bugs, and mother yelled at me to get rid of them. "What are those?" This one seemed to have tusks with claws at the end.

"His mandibles. Impressive, huh?"

I examined both sides of the creature.

Sam asked, "Do you like it?"

I loved it but needed to be firm with Sam. I placed it in the middle of the table. "I can't accept. I appreciate the gesture, but we're going to a hotel to hotly screw, I hope. That's why we're here. Nothing more."

Sam didn't flinch. He didn't redden. Instead, it was worse. He looked at me with disappointment.

I stood. "I think we should—"

"Please!" He jumped to his feet. "Please stay. I've overstepped."

I waited until he sat again, had rewrapped the gift, and returned it to his bag.

Neither of us said a word. After a few minutes, he began a conversation about Paris, assuming I'd been there. I feigned ignorance and told him I'd never been to the City of Light.

"Really? I could have sworn you had."

"Why is that?"

"I don't know. Just a feeling."

Thankfully, the waitress came and asked if we'd like dessert. I'd eaten very little. The waitress scowled down at my dish and was about to say something, but didn't after looking at my expression. Sam ordered us dessert and coffee. I sat back, twisting my napkin.

Sam asked, "Are you OK?"

"I'm sorry. Excuse me." In the ladies room, I checked both phones. No message from home. None from Snoop. I hated the smell of bathrooms. I took a Pepcid, held onto the sink, and waited for the nausea to pass. I was running on nerves and caffeine.

Back at the table, the coffee and our shared crème brûlée had arrived. Sam handed me one of two spoons and insisted I break the crust. I dipped into the pudding. When it landed on my tongue, I groaned. Embarrassed, I said, "This is the best I've ever tasted."

Sam smiled in agreement.

I met his eyes. "You're too nice to be doing this."

He shrugged. "I'm a romantic. What can I say?"

I could like this guy. But I had also been attracted to Gerard. "I'd say you've been on the wrong dating site."

I recalled saying this to another date. God, now I was repeating myself.

Sam said, "You're the most beautiful woman in the restaurant."

When I set down my spoon, I remembered spoon-feeding Hank.

Sam smiled. Maybe he meant it.

I liked this guy's quirkiness and sensitivity, how he was attractive but not conventionally handsome. But he was also just too ... too sensitive. Not that I was looking for anyone.

I was just lonely, and that made me vulnerable. I didn't moon over guys. That was what my sister used to do. I was a cynic. What was the definition I'd once heard? Oh, yes. A cynic was a romantic who had had their heart broken.

I wiped my mouth on the napkin. "Time to go." I left the restaurant ahead of him. Outside on the street, I lit a cigarette. My hands shook, and I tried not to scream in utter frustration.

37

As Sam unlocked the door to #721, I stood tall and strode into the room as if I owned it. Hank's survival depended on me being tough. I'd broken my own rule by going to dinner. Now I'd pay for it. These dates were affairs, and affairs were for sex. Sam knew what he'd signed up for from the beginning.

The real truth, of course, was he *didn't* know what was coming. I was worried now about how he'd handle the demand for money. I worried about how I'd deal with his reaction. I didn't want to hurt him, but I would. I blackmailed adulterers. That's what I did. I was no longer fighting for justice—I was fighting for my own personal gain just like every other criminal out there.

So get used to it. You're amoral. You're a piece of shit.

I thought of Steve, of our night, how weird it was. Maybe I should text him, meet up, and give it a go again so I could demand the money. Thank god I had no video of us having sex—if that embarrassing session could even be considered sex.

No. Scratch that. Steve had met up with Conrad. That was enough to nix any communication.

Sam chattered as he walked around the room. I was surprised by the way his body moved. Sexy.

"I ordered champagne. Hope you don't mind." Sam asked.

Champagne. Not again. I turned away, grabbed a hotel bathrobe from the closet, and took my small bag into the bathroom.

Jesus. This was torture. If I saw Sam on a regular basis, he'd probably call me his *paramour*. He'd probably read poetry to me, too. When I demanded money from him that should kill his romantic notions. Like a swatter to a fly.

My stomach turned. I was not heartless. I was not cruel. But if I ever went to court for Gerard's murder, the jury would see me as the worst of humans.

So, here I was, thinking about killing Sam's romantic inclinations with blackmail. Guys like him were rare. What was wrong with me?

I came out of the bathroom, makeup washed away, hair brushed back, bathrobe cocooning my body.

Sam's eyes bugged out. "Uh, wow. You look like a starlet."

He liked me *without* makeup, too? I couldn't help but laugh. "Starlet? You've watched too many movies."

"I love movies, especially classics. Do you?"

I remembered watching old movies with Sophie on our movie nights, and my chest filled.

Sam said, "One of my favorites is *Vertigo* with Kim Novak. An underrated actress in my humble opinion."

That had been Sophie's favorite old film. The hand of paranoia grabbed at my throat. What was the possibility? For a second I wondered if he knew more about me than he should. But why would he? What if he had a hacker, maybe named Mole, digging around in the dirt for info on his dates? Jesus, this sucked.

Time to get to work. The bed was turned down. I sat on the round edge to rub lotion onto my legs and thighs, something that usually turned on the shy ones. I said to myself, *I am not a whore. This is for Hank.* A moment later, I found a small package, "Essence of Vali." I read further. "A Bedtime Ritual." I pulled the vial from the card, the stopper from the vial. Lavender filled my nose, along with the scent of cedar wood. When I turned the card over, it read, "SLEEP."

Oh, how I wished.

"Do you know *Vertigo*?" he asked.

"What?"

The *pop-pop* sound of Snapchat from my phone. Snoop. I struggled to read her message. She'd once told me Ashley Madison filled the site with fembots. A fraudulent practice, so men paid for more chats. "Lowdown shit," she'd called it. Her message said she'd vetted two more names. I muted my phone and put it back on the bedside table. I couldn't do another date. I just couldn't. I had to go through with Sam tonight, get 10K from him.

I looked up. Sam stood over me.

38

"You OK, Claire?" Sam held out a glass of vodka on ice. I took it. He sat on the edge of the bed and placed a hand on my leg, even though he was still looking at my face.

"Of course I'm OK." I lifted my glass to him and took a drink. His hand now slid up to my thigh. I finished the vodka and opened my legs a little. Now he did look down.

But only for a second. He looked up into my eyes and said, "Sure you're OK? Maybe we shouldn't."

That jerked me back to reality. I laughed. A harsh trumpet of a laugh. A crazy sound even to me. I said, "This ain't my first rodeo, Sam."

"Why are you doing this?"

"Jesus! What are you a psychologist?"

"No. A coleopterist."

"What?" What was he talking about? I closed my eyes. When I opened them, he pointed at the graphic on his shirt, a beetle of some kind.

I pushed off the bed, walked over to the curtains, and pulled one aside. My breathing felt jagged. My heart pounded against my ribs. My nerves were collapsing. Hank was going to die. All the doctors said so. But the operation *could* save him. His odds weren't good, but I had to try.

I felt Sam behind me.

"You smell like buttered toast." He kissed the back of my neck.

Outside dusk had settled. City lights flickered. Something clawed at my chest. My throat tightened like I was being strangled.

He kissed my neck again. I turned and shouted, "Stop! Stop pushing me! I'm not going to fall in love with you, damn it."

I tried to shove past, he grabbed me, pulled me to him, but I broke free. As I walked backward, I held up my palms and hissed, "Don't. Don't even think about it."

He looked upset.

"Listen to me," I said, softening my voice. "I don't want romance, tenderness or understanding, OK? I want to fuck and go home. If you don't want that, too, then I'll leave."

For a moment, he said nothing. His mouth turned hard for a second before softening. "OK," he said. "I understand."

I walked to the bed and turned to face him.

He approached me. I had to look up. I realized for the first time how much taller he was than me. He slowly reached under my robe, ran his hands up the back of my thighs to my buttocks, and lifted me onto the bed where he forced me down, his knees on each side of my waist. He grabbed my wrists and pressed them over my head. I hadn't expected this. Not from shy Sam. Not from nervous Sam. When I tried to escape, he gripped tighter. I glared at him, trying to hide an edge of panic. He bent down, pressed his mouth to mine, and opened my lips with his tongue. I shivered. Damn kisses. I kissed him in return. Tongue to tongue, nibbling his lips. He tasted good. Not many men did.

He released my wrists, peeled back my robe, licked my breasts, bit my nipples, kissed my stomach and pelvis, leaving heated circles on my skin. My nipples burned. I arched up when he went down on me, and I opened my legs wide, forgetting everything as I wildly shuddered. And I'd done nothing for him.

My body and brain crumpled. I caught him staring at me. Unsmiling. What did he see when looked down at me? He skimmed off his shirt and snaked off his belt. He undid his zipper, and now I knew we *would* fuck. He grabbed me by the buttocks again and pulled me down. He still wore his watch, the crystal flashing in the low light. I sharply inhaled as he entered me. He pulled my hair away from my face, holding it tightly at the nape of my neck, forcing my face to his. His eyes darkened. His mouth tightened, as he slowly ground into me. "Is this what you wanted?" He yanked my head back. "Is it?"

Yes. No.

My body clenched again, and I groaned and closed my eyes. Then he flipped me over and pulled me up and entered me again. When he came, he hissed.

We both collapsed, panting.

We laid there saying nothing. I was sore. I pulled my robe closed. Sam rolled away, and I sat up. We didn't talk. He brought me water and vodka. We sat in bed and devoured crackers and cheese. But something was different. Sam was different. I thought he'd be an over-eager, asexual male who would be a disappointment in bed, but not anymore. Right now he looked alpha and very sexy.

A phone rang.

I slid out of bed and picked up my cell, hand trembling.

Hank? But it wasn't my phone. I'd muted it. I turned the volume back on.

Sam sat on the edge of the bed, cell to ear. His elbows on knees, one hand to forehead, straight back curved under what he was hearing. When he looked up, he said, "I'm sorry. My wife has asked me to come home. I need to go."

"Is she OK?" Nothing except her dying would have justified him leaving. But of course, she didn't know what we were doing. Or did she?

"I'll soon find out."

Perspiration glistened on my body. It cooled. I shivered. Sam now returned to the anxious, unsure date he started out as. Jumping to his wife's demand brought me back to reality. I needed to demand the 10K. "Why do you have to run off?"

He grabbed his clothes off the floor and started to dress. He was agitated. "I'm sorry, Claire. I don't want to go," he said in a pitiful voice, "but I have to."

"I need to talk to you."

"Not now."

I plunked down on the bed, pulled my knees up to my chin, and said, "So I'm just a fuck." I hated how I sounded, but I was angry. Yet hadn't it been me who'd said this date was for sex, that was all?

Sam took my face between his hands and kissed me, softly, sweetly. "Thank you," he said. "I'll call you." Then he grabbed his duffel and was gone.

39

I couldn't sleep, so I dressed, grabbed my smokes, and took the elevator to the hotel roof, where I leaned on the concrete rail that surrounded the upper parking lot. The rain had stopped, but a chilly wind whipped my hair. I had trouble lighting my cigarette.

Hank and I had stood right here, too, after tearing up the round bed with our lovemaking. We'd kissed, couldn't stop touching each other, kissed over and over. Both of us had been amped, our bodies cranked with new love and possibilities. We walked the streets. Cities were romantic at night, and we kissed on every corner and in dark nooks. He'd had this certain way of holding me when we kissed, one hand at the back of my head, the other pressing on the small of my back.

Kisses. Why were they so damn powerful? The men I'd dated from Ashley Madison rarely kissed. When they had kissed me, I felt nothing. But with Sam. ...

"Sam's gone," I said aloud, "and you got what you wanted." I had the video so I could demand the money over coffee or even the phone. End of story.

Strands of hair blew against my face and caught the lit tip of my cigarette. I dropped the cigarette and slapped the burning, fizzled hair.

But maybe he'd gotten what he'd wanted, too. Maybe that was the way he did it. Maybe that was his M.O. He acted the romantic and gets a good fuck, then at a particular time, the phone rings so he could escape.

I crushed the cigarette under my shoe and headed back to the hotel room. Screw Sam. I was done with this dating-blackmail scene, which meant putting the pressure on Hank's schmuck of a lawyer. I'd never know why Hank trusted him. Right after Hank's accident, he'd called me to his office. "I want you to stay out of this settlement with the business. I know you're a lawyer, but I won't put up with being second-guessed or micro-managed." I hadn't liked his tone or his threat, but I'd been too upset about Hank.

Back in the room, I grabbed a blanket off the bed and curled up in a chair. I woke at 4:45 when my cell rang.

It was Carmen, Hank's nurse. "Hank's failing. I wasn't able to get him to the hospital in time."

Hank had autonomic dysreflexia, impacted bowels that caused a massive spike in blood pressure and could be deadly if not treated right away. Carmen had always been able to catch it in time.

I popped a med, dressed, put the fake digital clock with the video into my bag, and packed. Then I called for my car and hurried downstairs. I slipped into the front seat, shakily lit a cigarette, popped a mint, and headed to Eugene to the hospital.

40

I checked myself in the mirror. Black heels, a black dress, cardigan, and pearls. That couldn't be me. I was glacial numb. The house was as lifeless as the Paris Catacombs.

Carmen, Hank's nurse, had taken his death hard. I gave her a memento, a chunk of iron pyrite, "fool's gold," that Hank had kept on his desk, a reminder that he was helping the world, not chasing money.

I searched for my purse and couldn't find it, found my cigarettes instead, and lit one. After Hank's fall and operations to brace his spine, the doctors hadn't held much hope of him surviving, never mind walking. Now I had to come to terms with the fact that I'd been wrong.

I'd thought Hank would live. Maybe I'd thought if I believed it with all my heart, he would live. After all the research, I fully believed that the operation in London that would give him mobility. The reports had encouraged me and given me hope. I just couldn't imagine him dying.

Hank and I had once talked about what we'd want if one

of us were to die. "Ang, I want a party for my friends and business associates."

I was dumbfounded. "You hate parties, Hank."

"It's not for me. It's for everyone else," he said. "No memorial. No celebration of life. Just a simple party where everyone can drink, eat, and tell stories about me—now that I'm dead." He had laughed. I hadn't.

An event room at a downtown restaurant and bar seemed big enough for forty to fifty people. Casual enough for a party. A side door where I could slip out to smoke. A large TV monitor. One of Hank's pals had created a slideshow. I'd given him home photos. Hank's elderly mentor, Caleb, contributed early business photos. I watched the slideshow at home before the party, and I cried until I felt sick.

I found my purse. It was on the kitchen counter where I usually left it. I realized I'd left a lit cigarette in Hank's office. I went back and stubbed it out. I saw Hank sitting in his chair, working on a formula with a pencil and large sheet of paper. He looked up and smiled at me. Then he was gone.

I arrived at the restaurant early, ordered a scotch, and checked that everything was ready to go. Half an hour later, people trickled in. I couldn't remember names. I should have bought name tags. People arrived from his Washington State R&D facility, even Caleb. He limped up to me using his cane, kissed my cheek, and told me how much Hank would be missed. He teared up. I helped him to a table and asked if he'd like a drink.

I ordered a ginger ale for Caleb from the hosted bar and took it to him. The kitchen delivered plates of finger food for each table. Back at the bar, I ordered another scotch. When I turned to greet some of the guests, the company lawyer intercepted me. "You hired your own lawyer? You're receiving a generous settlement from the business."

I hadn't invited him to this gathering. I was cold, inside and out. "This is not the appropriate time or place. Talk to my lawyer."

"But I don't understand. You said you needed the money and everything's in order, although it will take time to finalize."

Everything was *not* in order. "I went through Hank's papers. His laptop. His emails and documents. I estimated what the settlement should be, what Hank was owed. He kept detailed notes, budgets, spreadsheets ... and files of your and his correspondence. Funny how some things don't jive with what you've told me."

His eyes chilled. "I did what Hank requested."

"Really?" I rattled the ice in my drink. "I have nothing more to say. Talk to my lawyer."

I walked away then noticed that everyone was watching the slideshow on the large monitor. I stopped. Photos of Hank and me. Hank, me and Sophie. Hank and Caleb. Early days. Hank in front of his first R&D facility, young, rugged, sexy Hank who looked more like a cowboy than a chemical engineer. Then Hank with that great smile and his new business suit. His awards. His patents. His factory in South Africa. His operation in China. Everyone was watching.

I ducked out the side door.

Outside, I lit up. A homeless man sat on the concrete, back to the wall, his dog laying next to him, its head on the man's leg. The dog looked well cared for. I gave the guy a cigarette and lit it.

The nearby garbage bin smelled of rot and mice. Farther down the alley, the fresh scent of dog feces. Then a waft of barbecue ribs. Nauseated, I walked to the street for fresh air. Even my cigarette tasted cleaner.

I had nothing left. Couples passed by. Families too. A few days ago, I had canceled Snoop's services. I missed her. Funny how she'd filled a void. Sam's page on Ashley Madison no longer existed. I took mine down, too.

A nearby club blasted "Tainted Love." I choked as I inhaled. Sophie had loved that song. Another irony. Even though my sister had betrayed me, I missed her. I missed the times before she died when I'd known her differently. Before Hank. Before Gerard.

Gerard. Why did he appear so clearly? Why didn't he fade?

Because you killed him, you stupid bitch.

Oh, god. I had to stop this. Time to pretend it hadn't happened if I were to remain sane.

41

The call came a month later while I was cleaning out Hank's office and boxing up all his personal effects for charity. Almost everything important for the business had been sent to the company's office and the rest sat in boxes waiting for FedEx. My personal belongings were in boxes in the living room or garage. I'd sold most of the furniture. A family with three children had bought the house.

When my lawyer called, it was what I suspected. They'd found irregularities in the company's books. Money was missing.

"Angeline, do you know of anyone else who had access to the company's accounts?"

I tried to think. "No, I don't. I'm ... I didn't even have access. What about Hank's lawyer?"

"He depended on reports from the company accountant, but now the accountant has come under investigation because he's been strung out on opioids. Sorry, Ang. I'm not sure how long it will take to straighten it out."

My brain tripped like a security system. I was almost broke, although I still had 40K's worth of blackmail money.

"Angeline, did you hear me?"

"Hank kept good records. He knew where the money was, what was going out, what was coming in, the budget, the grants, the ... how could he not know about it?"

"Most of the loss took place while he was in China. It happened quickly and efficiently. With so many sub-accounts, it wasn't hard to skim off here and there and juggle the books."

I sat on a kitchen stool and lit another cigarette. "How much is gone?"

"Over a million."

"*What*?" My shout echoed in the empty house.

"Look, I'll be able to take care of you. Hank owns the patents and what the patents earn will go to you in perpetuity unless you sell them to the business. We need to talk about that."

"OK. Will I be able to live on what I receive? Is it—"

"It's a lot of shekels," Arthur said. Then he added, "But I'm afraid you won't see the bulk of it until the case is solved."

"Solved?"

"Yes. The case has gone to the Feds. They think it's part of a larger investigation they've had on their radar." Silence. "I'm sorry, Angeline. Really. I'm trying. I'll see what I can do."

I didn't tell him about the stash of 40K from my dates or the remaining 10K from the sale of the house. Until the investigation was finished, they were giving me a meager stipend. That was something.

After we hung up, I stepped out back into the untended

garden for some fresh air. I used to love this little oasis of color and scent. Now it reminded me of how far I'd fallen. Like the lilac that split during the winter and lay on the ground.

I shivered in my sweats. A thick fog had settled in the valley and hung over Eugene. My mind had the same problem. I was alone and had no one to call.

I'd cut back on the meds, so I'd been able to think more clearly even though I didn't sleep well. I was smoking more.

Working backward, I went over what I knew, and what had happened over the past two years, letting my mind wander and my lawyer's instinct rise to the top.

The money had disappeared while Hank was in China. He probably hadn't kept tabs on the accounts because he'd had sporadic internet and no wifi. The only people who had access to the accounts were Hank, Caleb—who couldn't be guilty because he had no financial acumen—and the accountant. That left the accountant. From what I knew from Snoop about hackers, they couldn't access financial accounts unless they worked from the inside.

Another trail. Hank said he went to China to escape Sophie. Sophie worked on his website which gave her access to his computer. While Hank was in China, Sophie hung herself. Direct cause?

These questions led to the other trail—Gerard. Was he and Sophie lovers? She told me they were. She'd showed me his photo. She talked about him. But that could have been a cover for her affair with Hank.

Unrelated images flashed. Gerard and me at dinner. At the French Chateau. At the Eiffel Tower on New Years, drinking champagne.

Stop. Think about Hank. I lit a cigarette.

Maybe Hank had been wrong. Maybe Sophie had loved Gerard and used Hank to make him jealous. If she'd loved

Hank, but he hadn't loved her, Sophie wouldn't kill herself because of that. Sophie had had plenty of lovers, some she professed to be madly in love with, and after they'd broken her heart, or she had dumped them, she survived. She'd also had three abortions. She'd wanted a child, but when the men disappeared, well. ...

I'd made her promise never to tell me about the abortions, but she couldn't stop from confessing everything. Now I was pacing the backyard.

I had to stay on track. Think *motive*. Maybe I was asking the wrong questions.

I reminded myself of the three main reasons for a criminal act: love, revenge, money.

I'd killed Gerard out of revenge. For love of Sophie.

But what about her motive for suicide?

I eliminated love. She'd never talked about or threatened suicide when her other relationships ended, no matter how messy.

I eliminated revenge. Who would she be committing revenge against in taking her life? Her lover? No. That leaves. ...

Money.

The cigarette burned my fingers. I flicked it into the birdbath. A blue jay screeched overhead.

First Gerard. But what did money have to do with Gerard? Gerard had been a government official. He had no money. Or had he? I searched for his obit. Nothing. I checked the government office where he worked. He wasn't listed. I Googled his address, ran his name in different forms. I'd been tempted to call his cell, but I hadn't wanted anything traced back to me. Sometimes I thought I didn't want to know. Sometimes I wondered if he'd ever existed.

In the empty house at the kitchen counter, I opened my

laptop and searched Gerard's name again. So much for motive. The more I'd tried to find out about Gerard, the more he seemed like a ghost. At one point, I'd thought of hiring Snoop but had been afraid of what I'd find. Had the police suspected foul play? Had they investigated? What happened to his body after he was found? The drug I'd given him would not show up in a tox screen or autopsy, but his death could have been labeled as suspicious, especially if witnesses came forward to say he'd been with a woman, and she'd fled the scene. I remembered the Muslim family that sat next to us. Had they been questioned? If they had, I doubted if they'd have anything to say. They hadn't been paying any attention to us.

Why was there no trace of him online?

The phone dinged. Another text from Steve.

"Can we meet? Just to talk. Whatever's convenient for you."

This didn't sound like him. This sounded like something else. I didn't care and deleted the text.

42

FedEx came to take more boxes to Hank's business, old files created before the use of computers. After FedEx left, I stood in the hall, taking in the empty house, the official end of my life with Hank.

Like a mental text message, I said aloud, "Big money causes criminal acts, like the theft of ... millions."

Jesus.

I looked up at the ceiling and closed my eyes. I pictured Hank and Sophie in our house, in Hank's office. Sophie wanted to help him with his website. That gave her access to his computer.

"Oh, Sophie. You wouldn't steal from Hank, would you?"

Sophie *could* have accessed Hank's passwords. I didn't think he'd give her the company account passwords, but maybe she had a way to—

A car passed the house and backfired. I jumped and raced to the living room window. A landscaping truck. I rubbed my chest then checked the front and back locks. I grabbed a bottle of water from the fridge.

When I'd closed Sophie's accounts and shut down her

business, she hadn't had any million dollars. She didn't even have enough to pay her rent. She lived from one account payment to another. She was abysmal at budgeting. Hank had offered to help her, but she'd refused. She'd never been in real financial trouble, so she'd had no motive for stealing, other than to make life easier. But Sophie had never done anything the easy way. She'd once said to me, "If it's not hard, it's not worth doing." I'd always taken that as a philosophy to justify her life, not something she aspired to.

She *had* been facing upcoming motherhood if she chose to. If it had been Hank's baby—but a vasectomy made that impossible—he would have helped her. Hank and I might have divorced or even stayed together, who knows, but he would have helped financially. Sophie knew that. If Gerard had been her only other lover, that meant Gerard was the father. She could have demanded money from him. But she didn't have to go through with the pregnancy either.

More and more, I faced the possibility that she'd stolen the money. But it had to be in another bank, in another country, and that wasn't easy to do now. I couldn't imagine Sophie finding out how to do that. Why not? She had the Internet. She could have had help. I should tell my lawyer, but what proof did I have?

In the kitchen, I stood in front of the fridge and ate cottage cheese from the container.

The beep beep beep of a truck backing up into the driveway raised the hair on my arms. Then I remembered St. Vinnies was coming for the donations.

The doorbell rang. The truck driver wanted to know what I had to donate. I opened the garage door and showed him the boxes to take, the boxes that held what used to be my life with Hank. After the truck left, I locked up again and sat out back with my suspicions. If Sophie had stolen Hank's passwords, had she done that to steal company money? If she had stolen the money, had she felt so guilty she'd hung herself? What if she hadn't been working alone? Maybe she'd done it for someone else. What if ... shit. What if Gerard had talked her into stealing the money for the two of them to run off together? What if he'd told her how to hide the money and had his name on whatever entity he'd set up? What if he took the money and cut her out of the equation? This all seemed too absurd, even for me who worked in criminal law.

But Gerard hadn't disappear. When I met him, he hadn't seemed to be living the high life. He seemed so regular. Only after I poisoned him had he seemed to disappear. So where was the money? What if Sophie hadn't had her name on wherever she sent it?

Enough. I was going around in circles. I needed more information.

I Snapchatted Snoop.

"Can you get me info on a Frenchman, Gerard Duvernet? He worked for the French government. I think he lived in Paris. 15th e. He died New Year's Eve 2015. Anything you can find."

"sure/want everything?"

"Everything, no matter how unimportant it might seem. See if you can find an obit, too."

Somehow that put me back in lawyer mode. Maybe now I wouldn't have to keep laptop binging on "The Americans."

I made a cup of coffee, poured in cream, and dosed it with sugar. The cell vibrated. It was the phone company telling me they'd disconnect the landline tomorrow. I had no idea what I was doing or where I was going. I'd like to live in a hotel for a week or two. I'd always wanted to live in downtown Portland with its vibrant cultural life, great restaurants, the riverfront park, but not now. Not when I associated it with Steve and Sam, and with Hank dying.

I checked my laptop and Googled Gerard's name again. An ad popped up. Images of palm trees, sandy beaches, sunsets, sailboats. I clicked on the ad.

43

"Hi, Claire, it's Sam."

I stood naked in my bedroom, confirming my reservations at an Airbnb casita in Todo Santos, Mexico and waiting for my two sets of casual clothes to dry. The rest were packed. The house sale had closed, money had transferred, mortgage was paid off, and the buyers would move in in three days. My luggage sat open on the bedroom floor. I'd been sleeping on a blow-up mattress.

"Sam," I said.

"Are you busy?"

I didn't know if I wanted to speak with him. He'd left Hotel deLuxe, no explanation.

"Claire, can you talk?"

Claire? Oh, damn, I'd forgotten. That had been my alias.

"I was hoping I could see you. For coffee or dinner."

I should have hung up.

"I'm sorry I had to run out on you that night. I want to explain. It's taken me a while to clear things up, but I'm free now."

Free? What exactly did that mean? My heart beat faster.

He wouldn't apologize if he knew what I was going to demand that night.

"Can we meet? What are you doing now?"

"Right now?"

"Yes."

I decided to tell the truth. "I'm standing naked in my bedroom, checking my laptop, and waiting for my clothes to dry. And, Sam? My name is Angeline, not Claire."

He chuckled. "I figured."

"Figured?" Hair rose on my arms.

"Angeline fits you much better."

Ah. "When did you want to get coffee?" I asked, veering away from dinner.

"Now."

"We shouldn't do this," I said. "I'll be forced to tell you some truths you might not want to hear."

"Try me."

"Can we meet this afternoon? I have things to do. Plus, my clothes are drying."

"You weren't kidding that you're naked?" I didn't respond. "How about three o'clock at ... where's a good place?"

"How about drinks. Marché Restaurant's bar, 5th and High. It's a marketplace. The bar is on the ground level. Did you drive down here from Portland?"

"I'll tell you all about it when I see you."

We hung up. Sam might not want anything to do with me after I divulged what I'd planned for our night together. I didn't want another man either. I was prepared to spend the rest of my life alone, my penance for Gerard.

The doorbell rang. I peeked through the curtains. A turquoise Thunderbird sat at the curb. What the hell! I moved away quickly and pressed my back against the wall. I would stay still until I heard the car pull away, but it didn't. How had he found me? And why? I'd shown no interest. But maybe that turned him on. I had trouble breathing and quietly inhaled and exhaled. Where was my car? Was the garage door open? No, I'd closed it. Could he tell I was home? How long would he sit there? Should I call the police?

"Jesus. Go out there and tell him to get lost."

As I headed to the door, the Thunderbird revved and, as it pulled away, tires squealed.

That asshole. I waited for Steve to come back. This was creepy. Especially knowing he'd been with Conrad at the deLuxe. Could that meeting with Conrad have had something to do with me? But how could it? I was on overload. Couldn't think.

Downstairs, in the laundry room, my clothes were dry, and I slipped on socks, jeans, camisole, and sweater. I folded the rest of the clothes with fumbling hands. I couldn't get to Todo Santos fast enough.

44

There was no sign of Steve as I left the house and drove down the street toward downtown to meet with Sam. I wondered where Steve was. I wondered if he'd check out the house again. My paranoia about the meeting between Steve and Conrad grew.

The streets seemed overcrowded with cars, and I realized I was in commuter traffic. I was so out of synch with the rest of the world. When I wasn't sleeping, I chased Sophie's mystery or Hank's missing money. I was a widow. I had no sibling. Without the two people I loved, I was just a wanderer, a nothing. No, that wasn't true. I was a murderer.

The closer I got to Sam, the safer I felt. I knew I shouldn't. I shouldn't feel safe just because he was a man, just because I thought he was a *good* guy.

Maybe he wasn't. I hadn't considered that. What did I know?

God, had I ever been this pathetic before?

When I turned into the parking lot, I suddenly realized I was meeting Sam at a French bar. Bad luck? Fuck it. I wasn't superstitious. Besides, bad luck had hounded me without a French flag draped over it.

I was a little early and, as I drove around the parking lot, looking for a space, I caught sight of Sam getting out of a beat-up Volvo, not a car I'd expected him to drive. He didn't see me. I cruised slowly into another section of the lot, saw a parking space ahead, and as I headed there, I passed Steve's parked Thunderbird. I slammed on the brake. He wasn't in the car.

I got the hell out of there. Across Pearl Street, I careened into an overflow parking lot and abruptly stopped. Now I was spooked. Why was Steve at the same place I was meeting Sam? Only one answer seemed logical—Steve found out about Sam and me and was stalking him too.

I wasn't sure what to do, but I sure as hell wasn't going into that bar. I was tired of trying to figure things out. It was my life—what was left of it anyway. And I was leaving.

Two days until I was out of here. Last night, lightning had flashed and lit up the house. Thunder boomed in the distance. Today, dark clouds, heavy with rain, threatened to let go their deluge. I needed sunshine.

I had a little more cash from selling the cars. I had my tickets to Todos Santos. I made reservations at the Crystal Hotel in Portland for one night and would catch my flight the next day. I called my lawyer to let him know I'd contact him after I landed someplace.

I could finally put the past behind me.

A knock at the door. I hesitated to look out the window. When I did, I saw a young man, soaking wet, standing there with something wrapped in a white plastic bag.

I opened the door.

"Hi. I'm Mrs. Fielding's grandson."

I must have look puzzled because he said, "You're Sophie's sister, right?"

I nodded. My lips went dry. I blinked.

"I'm so sorry about Sophie. She was nice." He shifted

from side to side. "My grandma was your sister's landlady. She had a stroke. My mom and I were cleaning out her things and found this addressed to you. Maybe there's an explanation inside."

He took an envelope from the plastic bag and handed it to me. Various stamps covered the right-hand corner for mailing. My hands went clammy and my legs weak.

"I'm sorry," he said again.

I nodded. Again. I couldn't find words. I wiped one hand on my slacks. Then the other. Finally, I managed to say, "Is your grandma OK?"

He visibly relaxed, probably wondering if I was going to be upset.

"My grandma is in a home."

"I'm so sorry."

Now he nodded.

"Thank you for bringing this to me." I held the envelope to my chest.

"OK," he said, then turned and left, driving off in a Volkswagen Beetle.

Inside, I turned in circles. No place to sit. I found a corner in what used to be Hank's den, sat on the floor, placed the envelope in front of me, and deliberated as to whether I should open it. It was thin, not much in it, a plain brown letter-size envelope. What was in it could change my plans, my life. I instinctively knew I was better off without it.

Curiosity won out. Maybe it wouldn't ruin my life. Maybe it could answer a few questions that would plague me forever without it.

I didn't know how long I sat, staring at my sister's handwriting of my name and address.

When I finally opened it, I pulled out a note.

Dearest Ang,

Well, I've done it this time. I'm in a situation I can't get out of. I can't tell you how horrible I feel. What I need you to know is that I never meant to harm you or Hank, but I'm afraid I have.

I'm sending a photo of the men who trapped me into stealing money from Hank's business. I had an affair with the Frenchman, and we fell in love. At least I did. But his pal roofied us, pulled us into a three-way, and videoed the sex. I told him I didn't care. Go ahead, ruin me, but I won't steal from my sister's husband's business. Then he threatened to harm you if I didn't go along with his scheme.

So I stole over a million from Hank's business (I won't tell you how). But you always used to say: "Don't let the bad guys win."

I've already ruined my life, so I figured I could at least do what you would have done—screw these guys. So I put the money in a different account and the info about it in a safe deposit box.

Enclosed, you'll find a photo of the two men, a key to the box with its location, and some info on both guys. Beware of them.

Jesus. Sophie hadn't only stolen the money, but she'd put me in danger? Didn't she realize that by killing herself, she'd made me the target? What kind of sister did that? Maybe she thought she was shielding me, but look where that went? If she weren't dead, I might have strangled her.

No. I wouldn't have. I'd known she had no common

sense. It was my fault for ignoring it or making excuses for her.

I pressed the letter on the floor and bent over to read the rest, not wanting to know more, but hungry for more—and the truth. Plus, the letter was all that remained of her.

> Yes, I know I'm pregnant, but I don't know who the father is because of the three way. I'm *afraid* of who the father is. What if the baby turns out like him? Stupid me. Always stupid me. I will miss you terribly if there is such a thing as an afterlife. I hope your relationship with Hank continues to be strong and that you both can find it in your hearts to forgive me.
>
> I'm having Mrs. Fielding send this a month or so after I'm gone. It will be hard enough for you dealing with losing me without adding this to it right away. I hope by then these two men will have gone away and given up.
>
> I love you and always will,
>
> Sophie

When I stopped crying, I was scared. Not only to pull the photo from the envelope, but scared for my life. Sophie hadn't thought it through as usual. Hadn't she known the men might come after me? That they'd figure Sophie had told me about them, even the money?

But maybe they thought she'd never stolen it. Maybe—I hoped—they thought she'd killed herself because she *couldn't* steal the money. Plus, I now realized Gerard *had been* guilty. He *had been* responsible for her death.

Oh, my god. All this time thinking I'd killed an innocent man.

I still had killed someone, but now at least I could say he deserved it.

Attached to the letter was an email from Hank to Sophie.

Sophie,

No, I don't care what you have to tell me. We are through. I'll always love you—as a sister-in-law, but I'm in love with Angeline. Don't text me again. Or email. You'll break your sister's heart if she finds out. You know how much she cares for you, has protected you.

I'll be out of the country for at least two months. Try to act normal, for God's sake. Get some Valium if you need it. Find someone else to fill your loneliness. But don't hurt your sister. She loves you.

So Sophie'd had the decency to prove to me that Hank wanted out. As if that mattered now.

I couldn't imagine who would be in the photo. My heart beat faster as I reached into the envelope. My stomach roiled. I felt the photo and slipped it into view.

I recognized Gerard on Sophie's right side. The photo appeared much like the one she'd first shown me, but with an addition. I drew the photo closer.

I thought I recognized the person on the other side of Sophie. I did, but I didn't want to. Sophie looked uncomfortable as he held her around the waist, tight to his side. Oh, god. What a fool I'd been. Talk about my sister having no sense. I'd been taken in by the same characteristics I always warned my clients about. Sometimes the most charming and sincere-seeming people committed the most amoral crimes. Sometimes they even seemed empathic. Instead, they saw your weakness and played into it. They knew what you needed and wanted before you did.

It was him.

It was Sam.

I didn't know how long I sat there, staring at the photo. The shock wrapped me in a blanket of nothing—no fear, no surprise, no warning, no anger. My brain tried to grasp what I was looking at, what the photo meant, but couldn't. Maybe if the other man had been Steve, even Conrad—anyone else —I wouldn't have been so horrified.

But Sam? The polite, almost shy guy across the table at St. Jack? The guy who had shown so much concern? The lover who awakened possibilities?

I was not on my game. I hadn't been in a long time. I'd been bamboozled, tricked, used. But no more.

46

I stayed up all night strategizing. I was back in charge. I wasn't going to let Sam get away with this. Like all the other white-collar criminals who'd never done time commensurate with their crimes, who'd never taken responsibility for ripping off life savings and the deaths they caused, the suicides, the heart attacks, Sam wasn't escaping retribution. Not this time.

I took a taxi to the bank where the safety deposit box was. After I showed ID, the papers Sophie left me, and her death certificate, I was escorted to a vault then left alone. I used the key and pulled out the only item, an envelope. Somehow, I'd turned into an observer of my life, the emotions sitting deep inside me like this vault. I accepted that I needed the distance and emotional removal, but sometimes I couldn't feel *me* in my body.

The papers in the envelope appeared to be for a business. Sophie was listed as the CEO and me as the Administrator of Finance. She'd named the company SoftCell Consulting

"Oh, Sophie!" I smiled at the inside joke. Soft Cell was

the name of the group that had recorded "Tainted Love." That proved to me that she alone set this up. So why? I read the note.

> Ang,
>
> I've set up a business account in Delaware. Unlike other states, Delaware never asks questions or records the name of the owners. The money I stole from Hank—and you—was transferred there a chunk at a time. Gerard and Carl (if that's his real name) set up an account for me there, so, figuring they know how to hide money, I followed suit. Soft Cell is my 'fake business' where I hid the money.

Carl? Was that Sam's real name? The note went on to tell me that I could either transfer the money back into Hank's business or use it as I saw fit. Only one signature was needed, not both, so I had control over the money. She gave me detailed instructions on how to place it in an international bank if the need arose. My sister, who was—had been—so terrible at planning and follow through, seemed to have finally found her niche.

Following her directions made the money accessible anywhere. I wore a money belt 24/7 with the account info. I considered burning my sister's info, instructions, and photo, but decided it was best to keep it if I ever needed to prove what happened to that money, or my sister, or. ... I couldn't foresee the future, but I'd seen enough cases where hard evidence would have made all the difference to the outcome.

Over the next two days, I bought a new cell phone with a

private number, plus a burner. I called my contact in San Francisco and arranged for a new identity. I'd need to change my hair, get fake glasses, and have a photo taken. I would go someplace tropical with my new identity. I'd have the money Sophie stole—easy to access with a code I'd set up—and my 50K. No need for lawyers and what they'd grant me after they settled the business. I didn't care. I'd live simply. Angeline Porter would no longer exist.

Sophie, even though she'd created this mess, had told the truth in the end. But with the money she'd stolen—*my* money, *our* money—I'd gladly buy back my sister if I could.

47

The shuttle took me to the Crystal Hotel in downtown Portland. It was my secret hotel, one I'd stayed at when I needed a break from work and home. The hotel rooms were named and decorated after famous musicians and musical groups. I hadn't been there in a while, so the desk clerks had changed. I checked in. The last time, I'd stayed in a corner room dedicated to the Decemberists, a bright, cheery room. This time I was in room 307, the Wilson Pickett Room where I settled in—as much as I could. The words to "In the Midnight Hour" wrapped around the walls. The black velvet draperies echoed my mood. Then again, the deep red hue of the walls also echoed my mood, the angry part. Add in the animal upholstery, and all my moods were covered.

I'd chosen this place after it opened because no one would think of looking for "straight" Angeline in a hotel with a rock'n'roll vibe. Not even my sister. At times, I'd needed a break from her, too.

A few minutes later, the walls closed in. Claustrophobic. Too small, too dark. I grabbed a coat and escaped. Outside, I lifted my face to the moist air. The rain had stopped, leaving the pavement shiny under streetlights and neon signs. From across the street at Jake's, the smell of seafood wafted over, but I wasn't hungry. From another restaurant with outdoor seating , cigarette smoke.

I headed to the river park, blocks away. At the riverside park, I sat on a bench, nerves tight and mind numb. I needed a med, but I was trying to cut back. The flow of traffic across the Burnside Bridge created a trail of lights. Along the expressway, horns honked, and emergency vehicles sounded in the distance. Teens walked by, loud and jostling, the stink of pot trailing them. I hugged myself, remembering those carefree days. If they only knew. But I was glad they didn't.

"Enjoy your freedom, young people," I said aloud, sounding old.

On my way back to the hotel, my chest tightened, and I stifled a moan. I'd had a good life. I hadn't caused any of this. I had my faults, but I wasn't guilty of this damned mess. At a trashcan, I threw away the photo of Sam, Sophie, and Gerard. Screw them. Screw them all.

I walked on, but then turned and rushed back and dug out the photo. I needed to keep my head. I needed to stay calm. I couldn't make mistakes or jeopardize my survival. I pulled out the photo, wiped off whatever clung to it, and shoved it into my purse. I needed this photo to remind me of what I was dealing with. I needed the image of that son-of-a-bitch Sam. Carl. Whatever.

The sidewalks filled with people. I glanced around to make sure I saw no one I knew. It was the after-work crowd. They bustled. They had a sense of direction. I had none. Just off Stark on 10th, I spotted a street-side window. A curtain behind it lit up in pink. Someone pulled the curtains aside and tied them back. *Pepe le Moko* was scripted on the glass. A pink neon sign at the bottom announced "cocktails."

I slipped into the small entry. Canned specialty goods filled corner walls. Ice-filled half-barrels showcased oysters. A young couple holding hands descended a narrow stairway. I followed to what looked like a bunker—a long room with brick walls and lit candles. A bar ran along one wall while small, round tables ran along the opposite. I took a table and leaned back, feeling myself relax. The dark bar had a calming effect.

I needed this respite. In between two worlds. I wanted companionship, yet I didn't. I wanted relief, but I wanted revenge more. I didn't know what to do.

Because of the poor light, I couldn't read the menu, so I ordered a Negroni and, as I sucked on the orange peel, I pulled the photo from my purse and held it up to the candle flame. I wanted to burn it, but it wasn't the photo I wanted to burn. It was Sam.

When I stood to leave, I threw a twenty on the table. Outside, I filled my lungs and felt my no-med strength return. Clear-headed and strong, although my nerves twinged. These men had used my sister and caused her suicide. They'd tried to use me. They were vultures that cared only for themselves and used fake kindness, fake understanding, fake emotions.

I'd lost my sister and husband because of these greedy, amoral fuck-heads. I no longer felt guilty for killing Gerard. Even if I died, I would keep Sam from hurting anyone else. I was Lady Justice.

It was obvious why Sam had hooked up with me—and why he'd wanted to keep seeing me. He'd come after money. Whether he suspected I knew about the money Sophie stole, or whether he later found out about Hank's death, it didn't matter. He was scum. He was a bottom feeder. If Sam thought he could console me, the rich, grieving widow, let him.

Sam didn't know about the packet Sophie'd left. That packet put power in my hands.

I was almost to the hotel, my brain on fire. I'd use Sam's methods against him. The law wouldn't help. There was no conclusive trail to Sam and no evidence to tie him to Sophie stealing the money. He probably knew how to cover his ass and let others take the fall. But this time he wouldn't get away with it. This time he was toast.

In my Wilson Pickett room, I pulled back the curtains to let light in, took the gun from my suitcase, and put it back in my purse. I wondered if Sam knew what had happened to Gerard. Then I wondered about their connection? Had Sam used Gerard? Or had Gerard been deep into this scheme?

I called Sam. My cell would pop up as a private name, private number on his phone. Still, he picked up right away.

"Sam, it's Angeline."

"Angeline! God, I've been worried about you."

He sounded so sincere. What a performance. I swallowed hard, made my voice sweet, and rambled excitedly. "Sam, I'm so sorry I didn't make our date ... my lawyer suddenly called to talk about my late husband's estate ... and I was so upset, I couldn't find your number. Then I accidentally trashed my phone."

I figured the word *estate* would make him sit up and salivate. I finished tempting him with, "I'm in Portland. Are you busy? Do you have time for drinks?"

We didn't chitchat. Instead, we arranged to meet at the Multnomah Whiskey Library around 10:00 p.m. That gave me a few hours. I called my contact in San Francisco from my burner. I gave him the code words. Yes, he had a person in Portland who could provide what I needed. Yes, within the hour. It would, of course, cost more. Fine. The package would be delivered to the front desk, wrapped and taped in a bag with my name on it. The envelope with cash needed to be addressed to "True Love Never Dies." I laughed then apologized. My contact asked if that was a problem. I said no, no problem. I didn't try to explain why "True Love Never Dies" was so funny. I doubted if I could.

My hand shook as I addressed a hotel envelope and placed the cash, five one-hundred-dollar bills, into it. On a sticky note, I wrote: "For pick up of package 'True Love Never Dies.' They would leave a package addressed to me."

I called the front desk and explained what I'd be doing so there was no problem with the exchange. "I'm a criminal lawyer, and I'm receiving info from an informant. It's important for the case I'm working. I'll give you my card, and you can call my office to check this." It was my old law firm. I'd be gone by the time they checked *if* they checked.

The clerk thanked me. Amazing what lawyers could get away with.

I changed into something a little sexy, not too much, more than when Sam and I had had our date. I added a little makeup. Could I do this again?

I wasn't sure. Even knowing Sam was a sick fuck I didn't know if I could go the distance without choking. This time it was more real.

Why hadn't I recognized Sam for who he was? I'd dealt with guys like him before. I had to give him credit—he was a class act and an intoxicating lover. This time I planned to play *him* like a perfectly tuned Stradivarius.

I hadn't heard back from Snoop. I needed to know more about Sam before I we met.

As I rode down the elevator, I gave myself a pep talk:

Sam couldn't ensnare me; he didn't know what I knew; I had the upper hand.

Still, Sam could kill to get what he wanted. He'd probably never had a twinge of regret when he heard that Sophie committed suicide. I'd bet the only thing he regretted was not getting the money.

At the desk, I gave the clerk my envelope, addressed to "True Love Never Dies." The clerk gave me a small, red cloth bag printed with "Keep Portland Radical." I laughed.

The desk clerk was a big boned gal with a great smile. "I wish I knew what your case is about."

"Sorry, I can't talk about it." I slipped the bag into my purse and then diverted attention. "I love Portland, but it seems crowded now. I remember what it used to be like."

Her hands went up in mock surrender. "Right? I know, I know. I can't even afford a starter house."

I nodded and sighed. "I wish we could turn back time."

She deflated like a punctured balloon and shook head as if to say there was no going back.

Another customer came in, wanting to know if any rooms were available. I took a deep breath and pushed through the doors, knowing tonight would be the last I spent here, not knowing where I'd end up. Tropical paradise? Jail?

On the sidewalk, I stopped. I could go back to my room. Forget all this shit. Go someplace and never look back. But I heard Sophie say, "You were always the brave one." When we were kids, she'd once called me her hero because I kidney punched a kid for bullying her on the bus. He'd crumpled to the ground. I hadn't thought of it as brave, just necessary.

I pulled the red bag from my purse. Inside the bag was bubble wrap that had been pressure or heat-sealed. I ripped it apart to reveal another small bag and inside that bag was a tiny brown bottle. Inside the bottle was the pill. I tucked the pill into my empty change purse. As I headed to 11th and Alder, I threw the packaging into a curbside bin.

Protecting Sophie had been my duty. For her, I'd be her hero again.

Quarter to ten. Outside the entry to the Multnomah Whiskey Library, I decided on an approach for tonight. I wanted the truth. I wanted the *who, what, where,* and with *whom*. The *why* was evident. Money.

The dark, narrow stairway to the second floor led to a door that could have been Prohibition era. Inside, the light was dim. I looked for Sam, or Carl, or whatever his name was, in case he'd come early too. The clientele appeared to be business people, entrepreneurs, and upper middle class. No beer swillers. No raucous voices. No TV monitors. Walls of liquor bottles to the ceiling. Dark wood. Club chairs. The place reeked of a vintage "men only" club, but there was an even mix of women and men. I liked it.

A handsome young man in a bowtie approached and asked if he could be of assistance. Then, from a distant club chair, I saw a head turn in my direction. Sam stood and waved. I thanked the young man, took a deep, ragged breath, and plastered on a smile. As I headed toward Sam, I hid my internal hate for him behind an exterior of real grief and confusion. His smile and friendly eyes could have fooled anyone. He was a pro. I'd give him that.

"Hi," I said in a raggedly emotional voice.

"Gosh, you sure look gorgeous. I never thought I'd see you again." He leaned in to kiss my cheek, but I jerked away.

"Sorry," I said. "I don't feel gorgeous. It's been a tough month."

"Please," he said as he pointed to the chair kitty-corner to his. A small table held his drink. "What can I order for you? Are you sure you're OK?"

I looked down at my purse and, without trying, a tear ran down my cheek. Jesus. Why couldn't he be the real thing?

"I'm still shaken by my husband's death and all the changes. I'm not very good company right now. I think it's catching up with me."

He reached out and took my hand. "You don't have to stay. Have a drink and then leave if you want. This is a difficult loss for you."

This was how he managed to get women to steal millions for him. No wonder Sophie had fallen for it. Now I wondered whom she fell for? She'd said it was a Frenchman. But Sam was more charming than Gerard. Even when I knew what a bastard he was.

"What can I get you? You like the clear alcohols, right? Vodka? Gin?"

I didn't know. I wasn't tracking, and that wasn't good.

"Can I order for you? Maybe a French 75? It's refreshing and bubbly."

Christ. Here we go with the bubbly again. "Yes, thank you."

When the drink arrived, I was surprised at how much I liked the French 75. This was one thing that made it impossible to reconcile Sam's two sides—the empath and the psychopath. He only used this side to get what he wanted. I have to remember this. But it was difficult. As I looked him over, it was also difficult to forget the sex we'd had.

"So what else is going on in your life, Claire ... I mean, Ang. I'm having trouble with that!" He laughed. "If I call you Claire, please remind me to call you Ang."

I nodded.

"You said you're dealing with the settlement of your husband's estate? That must be difficult and stressful. How far along are you?"

Ah. Now we were getting down to business.

"The lawyers are close to a settlement." Then I baited him. "But I've had to use my sister's money to get through. She left me a sizable amount. She committed suicide. I don't know if you know that."

Seeing his face was all I need. He couldn't hide the first glint of greed, which quickly morphed into fake concern. He leaned forward, placed a hand on my knee, and said, "No. I didn't. I can't tell you how sorry I am. You *have* been through hell."

"Yes. First my sister, then my husband." I paused for effect. "I have no idea where my sister's money came from." When I reached for my drink, my hand trembled. I didn't have to fake that. I took a sip.

A long silence ensued, and now I was frightened. I looked down with what I could only say was my version of sadness.

He said, "That's odd. How much money did she have?"

"You won't believe this. My sister had a million dollars."

I'd made a mistake. This was too direct. An obvious bait.

His eyes narrowed and glinted. He folded his hands in his lap. "How can you not know where it came from? All money can be traced. All money leaves a trail. Unless of course, the money is in a Swiss bank or offshore account."

I shook my head as if this was all too much. "I don't want to talk about the money."

He wasn't falling for it. He said in a quiet and bemused voice, "You're a lousy actress, Angeline."

I sat back in my chair, trying to look hurt. He smiled. That scared me more. Quickly, I figured he'd known all along about Sophie being my sister. He'd been playing me.

I sighed and sipped my drink. Sam sipped his. Each of us eyeing each other. I ditched my fake persona—which I guess I wasn't good at—and he revealed his true self, his con-man expression, so confident and assured. The twisted downturn to his mouth that had given me pause when I first saw it. A glimpse of his true nature I'd caught once or twice now showed clearly, void of conscience.

I reached into my bag and grabbed my change purse.

"Please don't do that. Take your hand away from your gun."

I snorted, unlady-like. "As if I'd shoot you in public." I gave him a big smile. I clasped the tiny purse in my hand and held it up. "My money purse."

The waiter stepped up to ask if we needed another drink.

Sam tried to send him away, but I said, "Hello, yes, please, only this time I'd like a double shot of vodka on the rocks, twist of lime."

He nodded. "Anything else?"

"Yes. I'd like to buy my friend a drink. Whatever is your best scotch." I was talking mucho bucks, like in the hundreds, but I didn't care. Sam tried to interrupt me, but I held up my hand. "Look, I have the money. *You* know that."

Sam gave a half smile. I turned to the waiter. He looked pleased. "Do you have a tab, Ma'am?"

I pulled out three one hundred dollar bills and handed it to him. "Will that cover it?"

"I'll be right back," he said, still beaming.

After the waiter left, Sam said, "You know I won't drink it."

"Really? Look, if you want to work with me, you'd better drink it and keep me alive. Or you won't have a chance of getting your hands on my sister's money."

He put his index fingers to his chin as if giving this thoughtful consideration. He waited. So did I.

Finally, I leaned forward and said, "OK. Let's get down to business ... Carl."

That shocked him. Carl must have been his real name because right now he looked like someone in a mug shot. Then he pulled it together.

"So ... do you know how much danger you're in right now?"

I studied him. "Why don't you tell me?"

He chuckled. "I like you. I like you a lot, Angeline. You've got balls."

"Is that a line from one of your vintage movies?"

"This is not a game. You know that."

"I'm a fucking lawyer. Do you think I don't know? What the hell do you want? I suppose you want my sister's money."

"You're not a lawyer. Not anymore. You've had your license revoked. What do I want? Yes, your sister's money." He studied his fingernails, which were well manicured. "I also want your inheritance. What you're going to get from your husband's estate."

"Oh, really?" I was thrown off by that. "What makes you

think I'd give it to you? Why wouldn't I go to the police or the FBI and report you?"

"Because you can't."

I tried not to visibly gulp. Did he know I killed Gerard?

"Because you've been blackmailing your 'dates' on Ashley Madison."

I wanted to let out a sigh of relief, but said instead, "Just how do you know that?"

"I have my ways."

"Another line from your vintage movies?" I waited, but he remained silent. "Look, if you're not careful, I won't give you shit. If you kill me, you won't get shit. So, here's my offer. I'll give you the million, but you leave the rest alone. You leave me alone."

"My French partner was supposed to convince your sister to steal the money, but he screwed the deal. I wouldn't be here right now if not for him."

This threw me. I took my time before saying, "So tell me about it."

"Gerard fell for his victim. He told me he was in love with your sister."

What? I couldn't make sense of it. Why would she steal the money then? Why, in her letter, had she accused Carl *and* Gerard of using her?

"Sophie was having an affair with my husband. They were in love with each other," I said, lying to see where he went with this.

"Sophie didn't love your husband," he said. "She fucked your husband *for* Gerard. She did it *all* for Gerard. She would have done anything for him."

Sure, Sophie might have stolen the money for love, but why kill herself if Gerard loved her? And why, when I had been with Gerard in Paris, had he acted so normal, even attracted to me?

"Sophie was as dick-whipped as Gerard was pussy-whipped," Carl said. I flinched. "When the three of us were at the Miami Business Fair, we went to my room Saturday night, and I slipped her and Gerard a little fun pill. The three-way was one of the best, ever." He paused. He looked like someone having a nostalgic moment.

The son-of-a-bitch. Doping her so he could fuck her?

"Bullshit," I spit out. "If Sophie and Gerard were in love, and you slipped them X, they'd be pissed. They would turn on you. They did, didn't they? They turned on you."

"Not exactly."

"Then how *exactly*?" I squeezed the purse in one hand.

"They tried to hide their relationship from me, but it was obvious, poor kids. After that Saturday night, Gerard told me he was done, wanted out of our business arrangement, and no way would he blackmail Sophie."

"And?"

"I told Gerard to get the money if he didn't want something very nasty to happen to her. He had to break it off with her, too, if he wanted to keep her alive."

"I know my sister. She wouldn't believe him."

"That's why I told her that Gerard had been using her to get the money. But you're right. She didn't believe me either, told me you couldn't fake real love, and they were going away together."

I imagined smashing my glass, jumping across the table, and cutting his throat with the jagged edge. Instead, I said, "Did you know that Sophie was pregnant?"

He nodded. "Unfortunate situation."

Now I knew I was going to kill him. "And that didn't bother you at all?"

"She didn't know who the father was—me or Gerard ... or your husband. But I have to say your sister was one tough bitch. To save Gerard, she took herself out of the equation."

I winced. "I'd like to roast you slowly over a spit, you son-of-a-bitch."

"I'm sure you would." He stopped for a moment. "Unfortunately, your sister wasn't very good at looking ahead. Her decision put you into the equation instead."

Then the whiskey came. Delivered by a different waiter who told Sam/Carl about the distiller, history, reason for this scotch whiskey being one of the best, etc. etc. While Carl was distracted, I tried to figure out how I'd drop the pill into the liquor. It wouldn't be easy. The waiter handed me the change from my three hundred dollars, and after folding it, I put the few bills in my change purse and took out the pill without Carl knowing.

After the waiter demonstrated the rich gold color of the scotch and waved it under his nose, he held it out for me to do the same. When I stood up to take the glass, I purposefully smashed my knee into the table and upset it. Vodka splashed onto Carl's slacks, and he jumped up. I grabbed the whiskey and slipped in the pill.

The waiter was now more concerned with Carl. Someone brought a damp cloth. After another employee righted the table and wiped it clean, I passed the whiskey to the waiter. When all was calm, he handed it to Carl. I received another vodka. Carl set the whiskey on the table.

After Carl and I sat down again and the waiters had gone, Carl's response of "Unfortunate situation" rang in my head. I tried not to look at the whiskey sitting on the table.

Carl finally said, "Sophie ruined our partnership."

Now I was all twisted up inside. I wanted to know what happened, but the pill was in the whiskey, and I wanted to watch Sam drink. I took a deep breath. "What happened to you and Gerard?"

"He knew I'd kill Sophie if he left. So he asked for a few months off to get over her and get his nerve back. I said 'sure' as long as he never contacted her again." Carl looked at the whiskey. Ah, now I knew he was tempted. "Then I heard from Sophie. She had the money, but would only give it to me if I didn't hurt Gerard."

"She never gave it to you."

"That's because Gerard called her, told her that he had used her to get the money, and he wasn't in love with her."

"How do you know he did that?"

"He told me. He figured he had to be mean and hurtful to her so she'd believe him. What a stupid dumb fuck. I knew she'd never give us the money then."

"And?"

"Your sister killed herself."

Silence.

My sister's death only made sense if she'd felt abandoned and used, so that probably was the reason. It also explained the letter. But something felt wrong. And it all went back to Gerard. Why, after Gerard died, had he disappeared, not a sign he'd ever been alive? Carl said nothing about that.

"I need to get out of here." I slugged down the vodka and stood.

"You don't want me to drink this?" He pointed to the whiskey.

"No. I don't give a shit what you do."

He picked up his jacket, slipped into it, and said, "OK. Let's go."

"I'm not going anywhere with you."

Before he could say anything, the waiter was there to see

if we needed anything else. Seeing us ready to leave, he looked down at the table, surprised. "You're not enjoying the whiskey?"

Carl picked it up, drank half, nodded in approval, and finished it, even licked his lips.

I kept my face neutral. "So what do you think?"

"Too expensive," he said. Nothing more.

I threw a tip on the table, and we left.

49

Outside, Carl grabbed my upper arm, fingers digging deep. His car was parked at the curb half a block away. "Nice touch with the old Volvo," I said.

At his car, I asked, "So what's with the Lesbian wife? Why did you leave that night in such a hurry?"

He pushed me against the car like a lover ready to smother me with kisses. People passed by. I wanted to scream for help, but I waited. The pill would kick in any time now.

Before I could stop him, Carl wrested my purse away.

"You don't need this." He took the gun and slipped it into his jacket pocket where it bulged and banged against my side. I tried to shove him, but he gripped both of my arms.

"You honestly want to know?" Somehow, he'd slipped back into his sweet Sam persona. It was unnerving. "I have a wife, but she's in this with me. She's bi-sexual, and we coordinate our encounters, her with women who are needy and wealthy and me with women who ... well, you know."

"Is she as good as you are?"

"You mean in bed?" He laughed, enjoying this. "Oh, God, yes. I'd fall for her if she made a pass at me."

I was getting scared. Why wasn't the pill working?

"You know what's sad, Carl? I love the good side of you."

"There *is* no good side of me. You should know that by now." He was back to being Carl. "I was a drama major. I created the good side." He touched my cheek as he pressed his body against mine. "Sure would like another fuck with you." Then he looked around, and when no one was in sight, he unlocked the car, took me to the passenger side, shoved me in, and locked it. I tried to get out. He wasn't showing any sign of dying. What if the pill was a dud? I banged on the door and pushed the lock, but nothing happened. Shit. I tried to scream and realized I couldn't. Panicked, I tried to get out his side, but he shoved me over. He heaved my purse over his shoulder onto the back seat.

I finally screamed, "Help! Help me!" but it wasn't a scream as much as a croak.

"Shut up," he hissed and smacked my head. I leaned against the door, tried the locks, the handle. Still nothing.

He started the car.

"Stop! Please stop! I'll get you the money."

Carl turned and smiled. "Of course you will. Or I'll cripple you like you did your husband." Sam's eyes brightened. I was speechless.

"I'd hate to do that. You're a pretty good fuck and—" His smile slipped, his eyes lost focus, and froth formed at his lips. "What the. ..."

Sam looked at me in surprise. He muttered, "whisky," then his eyes rolled back, his body jerked like he was being electrocuted, and he slumped against the steering wheel.

Outside, a lively group passed by and paid no attention to the car. I pushed Sam's head back against the headrest, but it fell forward again. I shut off the engine and took the keys. Trembling, I unlocked the car, wiped off the keys, the door handle and lock, left the keys on the driver's side door as if he'd dropped them, and retrieved my handbag from the back seat. As I backed out of the car, I remembered the gun, took it from Carl's pocket, and put it in my purse. Then I pulled his body down onto the passenger's seat as if he were sleeping.

My legs were weak as I closed the car's door. I stood for a moment to make sure I could walk then took an unsteady step, then another. I hadn't left ID at the bar. They didn't have my credit card. I'd used cash. I told myself these things in order to breathe. I had no idea if he'd left ID there, but that didn't matter. When I was sure I could, I walked briskly, but naturally, toward the Crystal, hoping I had enough time to get out of town.

50

N o one was at the desk. I got on the elevator and struggled not to cry. In my room, I packed and called an Uber. At the airport, I bought a first class ticket on a flight to San Francisco.

On the flight, I took the airline's magazine from the seat in front of me and opened it to an ad: "Escape! Come to beautiful Kauai." The photos showed a deserted beach, lush green and black rock cliffs, boats bobbing on a perfect ocean, sea turtles, and a couple drinking Mojitos under a beach umbrella.

After the short flight, I took the shuttle to a nearby hotel, where I Googled Kauai and another ad popped up, this time for Waimea Plantation Cottages outside Poipu. Why not? Once again, I wasn't going to Todos Santos. I'd leave a false trail.

I was betting that if anyone went looking for me, they would think I'd choose to escape to another country. At least that's what I'd assume if I were law enforcement.

Once again, I'd get a new ID, and after that a credit card and PayPal account.

If anyone did find me and wanted to arrest me for ... for what? But if they did for whatever reason, I'd say I had no choice but to escape because Sam/Carl's gang had threatened to kill me. They couldn't tie me to Carl's death unless someone identified me at the Whiskey Library.

But I was almost beyond caring. I'd killed the son-of-a-bitch responsible for Sophie's death.

51

The only baggage I had for my flight to Kauai was a backpack. I had a month-long reservation at Waimea Plantation Cottages under my new name River (an androgynous boho first name) Atwood (my favorite writer).

I had spiky red hair and large geeky glasses, and I'd whited out my lips. Fingerprint matchups were still more accurate than Facial Recognition Software, and most CCTV captured only grainy photos so matching me with facial recognition would be difficult, if not impossible. Carl—RIP —may not have thought me a convincing actress, but he'd never say that now.

He'd never say anything now. Or later.

I'd created an entire background and character for myself. As a writer from Connecticut with a trust fund, I swam, hiked, and ate organic. I wasn't talkative. I liked to wear next to nothing, maybe bathing suits with a sarong type covering. I wore shell necklaces but no other jewelry. In Kauai, my bare feet would harden. I'd get sunburned then turn brown. If anyone asked me about my past, I'd say I had none, only the present. If anyone pushed for info, I'd let tears fall and say, "I can't talk about it."

I'd swim, gather seaweed, and spearfish. Everywhere I went, I'd take my copy of Thich Nhat Hanh's *Power*, a book that I'd hoped would change my direction, and I would leave it on my chaise longue or beach towel when I swam. No romance novels for me. I wanted to change. I wanted to escape and start over—clean, fresh, like a newborn.

I slept for the rest of the flight until the plane approached the islands. When we came in for a landing, everyone chattered, smiled and laughed. Everyone expected to have leis laid over their head. I smelled salt water, although I knew that was impossible. I was nearly there. I had a feeling of weightlessness, of baggage left behind, of life opening up.

When I walked off the airplane and into the terminal, the scent of plumeria and tuberose filled the air. I had one flight until freedom, from the big island to Kauai. As I passed a trash bin, I threw away my meds. In a shop, I bought bottled water and my first necklace of tiny pink shells.

PART III

I picked up a stick and dragged it along the sand as I walked the beach, skirting the incoming waves, hoping to forget the nightmares that persisted even though I now lived in this small paradise. I had nothing to fear. I'd seen to that. Or so I told myself.

The mist retreated and surfers headed into the waves, unfazed by the lazy ocean. Half a dozen tourists spread out across the sand. A couple with a child built a sandcastle. Another quiet day.

My days were routine. I didn't know the date, only the day of the week. The sunburned skin on my shoulders flaked. My feet were calloused. I smelled of sunblock and sweat. My white cotton wrap flapped in the breeze and my worn jeans reached just below the knees. Now that morning had diffused, I slipped on my sandals and headed back to Waimea Plantation in the beat-up panel delivery wagon I'd bought from an islander who taught me to spearfish and how to collect edible seaweed.

Waimea Plantation was a step back in time. I'd been here for almost a month like a castaway who lived alone on a black sand beach. The central garden lead to where I parked a short distance from my one-bedroom cottage at the east end of the plantation. Palms and acacia trees surrounded my cottage on three sides, hiding it from view. Even though I read *The Garden Island,* Kauai's newspaper, the news from the mainland—destruction from mass shootings, hurricanes, floods, fires, the White House—seemed to come from another place and time, even a different country.

Angeline Porter no longer existed. I had fully taken on my new identity. Sun and sand had done that for me. Oh, and also the dogs.

I grabbed my beach bag and locked the car. A maintenance man waved. I waved back. Cleaning up my act hadn't been easy. Giving up anti-anxiety meds had been tough, but cigarettes? That had been so fucking hard, the worst. But I wouldn't give up my evening cocktails. Period.

I could hear Hank say, "Ang, you need to learn moderation."

"But Hank," I said aloud, "you know me. I'm not a moderate kind of gal."

I still talked to myself.

Five dogs greeted me at my front porch steps. They were a mangy, mixed-breed pack, typical of the island's abandoned mutts. I patted them and passed out jerky treats.

Hank and I hadn't had pets. Never had time. When my sister Sophie and I were growing up, Father had wanted a dog, but Mother refused. She hated housekeeping, and dogs were dirty fleabags that ate disgusting stuff and puked on your living room rug.

I was making up for lost time. During the first week at the plantation, these five mongrels had gathered on my porch. I fed them, something I was told not to do. But they were good company, my only company. The Plantation manager hadn't said anything because, maybe, when the dogs were with me, they didn't bother the other guests. Like me, they were alone and unsure, suspicious of strangers, ill-tempered when challenged, taking nourishment wherever. They were the only friends I wanted.

53

It was 3:00 a.m. A cloud-buried moon created a shrouded horizon. The dogs lay at my feet on the porch. Wrapped in a blanket with a glass of warm coconut milk in hand, I shook from tonight's bad dream, not my first. The nightmares had begun after I threw away the meds. Tonight I wished I hadn't.

The nightmares went something like this. Sophie phoned me. "Help, Ang. Help." Her voice, so familiar, but young. "Come get me. Please!" she said. I dropped the phone and headed her way. Like I always had. Sophie was at a rave, people high on something, lights pulsing to the music. I found her in the bathroom, curled on the floor of a cubicle, crying and terrified. I reached out to hold her. But my hands slipped through her, and no matter how I tried to lift her, I couldn't.

Sophie had never been to a rave, not her style. But I guess the dream had created a rape I could understand, a young man she might have a crush on, another young man who had a crush on her. I didn't want it to be a father with a daughter, a man who had raped Sophie just down the hall from his own daughter, a man we called a friend at a home where Sophie should have been safe.

I forced myself awake. Usually I would read until I was sleepy, but tonight, I couldn't.

Tonight's nightmare had been different.

I'd walked into Sophie's house for a night of movies, popcorn, and cherry sodas, but I couldn't find her. I searched everywhere. I headed for the door but heard her calling me. "Ang. *Ang!*" In the living room, Sophie swung from a noose in that blue dress, just as I'd found her. Only she was talking to me as if she were alive. Her face, however, her face was dead.

I'd woken up choking on my sobs. I hadn't saved her.

One of the dogs placed his head on my foot as I cried.

Hanging herself had been no solution. I *could* have helped Sophie. I could have forgiven her for the affair with my husband. I knew what she was like. She'd be alive. Hank would be alive. I'd have them both back.

Or so I told myself.

It was still dark when I woke in the chair on the porch. A quarter moon in a clear sky illuminated the ocean, the beach, the porch. My neck hurt, and I'd spilled the milk, but the dogs took care of that. Tempest, the only mutt I'd named, sat next to my chair with ears alert, growling. Two of the other dogs sat out front, looking up the beach. I patted Tempest. "What, girl?" But her attention was elsewhere. Her nostrils flared. I heard a rustle in the bushes to my right and stood, my heart racing. Tempest slipped down the stairs and into the underbrush. Probably a wild animal or another dog, but my mind went to Steve, how he'd stalked me in his turquoise Thunderbird before I'd come to Kauai. I'd never known why. I knew it wasn't for sex, though.

I headed inside, locked the door, then checked my

burner phone. In San Francisco, I'd smashed my other phone and trashed it at the airport. I hadn't brought my laptop, so I was unplugged. But with that came a sense of being dead, a ghost, someone who didn't exist in the larger world, a shadow of myself.

Funny how the mind worked. Take away all the distractions, the worries, the past, and the fears—like expecting the police to show up and arrest me for killing Gerard or Sam—and it didn't bring peace. My mind instead had gone deep and dark, digging up anger, anguish, ugliness, and all the events I thought I'd buried.

I wasn't talking about killing Sam who had planned to kill me. A case of self-defense. I was talking about killing Gerard. Even though he hadn't been innocent, I understood why Sophie loved him. Since moving to the island, my emotions and instincts were raw, like there were no walls between me and reality, no legal persona to hide behind.

But I'd been wrong about so many things.

I opened the screen door and flipped on the porch light. Four of the dogs were back. Tempest wasn't.

54

Every hour or two, I woke to check the porch. Finally, around sunrise, Tempest was back. I couldn't breathe. She was fearless, so I worried about her. Plus, I shouldn't have given her a name, shouldn't have given her affection. Those who loved me died.

It was too late to go to the beach, and I didn't have the energy to hike. A few days a week, I spent time at different beaches, then ate lunch or dinner, trying to avoid the tourist places like Brenneke's at Poipu, even though I loved their cocktails. Other days, I hiked but only those places that didn't have ravines or cliffs. I hated heights. I was happier studying the island's flora and fauna. I was a regular at the library where I researched the island. One of the librarians, Iolana, helped me. I liked her. She was older, motherly, and guided me in navigating the island's customs so that I didn't come across like too much of a *haole,* or worse, a tourist.

The fridge held nothing of interest, so I grabbed my bag and headed to Ishihara Market for fruit, poke, and a bento box. A few of the clerks knew me by name and greeted me.

"Aloha, River." I smiled and politely said, "Aloha," but didn't invite conversation.

Back at the Plantation, I pulled up, shut off the engine, and heard the dogs going crazy. Shit. Two of the dogs sniffed and prowled around the cottage. Tempest stood on the top step, growling, low and threatening, hackles raised. Not even last night was she like this. I let Tempest into the cottage and dropped the jute grocery basket on the kitchen counter. Two dogs raced off the porch, barking. I followed. When I looked up the beach, a tall, shadowy figure disappeared between cottages. I raced toward the spot, but I was too late. No one was there.

Back at my place, Tempest stood on the porch. Her eyes glinted and her lips were drawn back.

"It's OK, girl." I was careful as I approached her. I held out my hand, palm up, and squatted. "Good girl. Good job." Tempest growled. I whispered, "That must have been scary, but he's gone now." I continued to say soothing words. Her mouth relaxed although deep in her throat, the growl continued. I moved my hand downward to the patch between her front legs and stroked her fur. She sniffed my arm. My touch soothed her. Finally, she shifted her eyes from the beach, and our eyes met. We remained locked onto each other, eye to eye. The deadly glint faded, her jaw dropped, her tongue loosened. She leaned her forehead against my chest. I said soothing words we both needed.

When I was inside, the other dogs returned to the porch, still agitated. I tried to squelch my gut feeling. I didn't want to be paranoid, yet my gut kept saying *Steve* but he didn't know where I was. Neither did the law. They couldn't pin Sam-Carl's death on me. That was behind me now. No more men from the past.

After I fed the dogs, I was restless. Aloha life had finally reached the point of boredom. My legal persona wanted attention. I wanted answers. I knew I should leave it alone, like not scratching a bug bite until it bled. But the urge wouldn't go away. The unanswered questions drove me crazy.

I paced the porch, making the dogs nervous, so I went inside. At my dining table, I took a sheet of paper and made a list of the questions that lingered.

- Was Sam going to kill me or scare me? (I'd bet on *kill* me.)
- Who was Steve? (somehow contact Snoop?)
- Who found Sam?
- Was anyone looking for me? (check online newspapers at the library)
- Had anyone reported me missing? (news online?)
- Would I be able to maintain this disguise and live on what I had? (I hoped so.)
- What happened to Hank's business? (My lawyer would know—if he's still my lawyer.)
- What would happen if someone found me? (Depends on who it is.)

Nothing sparked any new ideas or answers. Snoop could help, but I couldn't contact her with my burner unless I called, and that was something I'd never done. Maybe I could find my former hometown paper online at the library and get some answers, but what good would it do me? Besides, I was a little scared of what I'd find.

No one knew what I'd been through. No one understood. At my law firm, no sex with the boss had meant no position, never mind partnership. I hadn't known that going in, and when I found out, I'd never dreamed I'd be targeted. I loved the law, but justice was blind, and it didn't always serve the righteous. At least I'd put that rapist away and saved a lot of women. I viewed it as a necessary sacrifice.

"But what about killing Gerard?" I said aloud as if presenting opening arguments.

Tempest scratched at the screen door. I let her in even though I wasn't supposed to. She curled up on the rug and fell asleep. Later, close to sunset, I took a martini, a beach chair, book, and notebook down to the black sand. Tempest followed. I hoped to see a green flash, an optical phenomenon that occurs on the horizon immediately after sunset. In my notebook where I noted Kauai's trees and flowers, I also tracked green flashes, the date and time of each. In one month, I'd seen three.

I loved that this was a black sand beach. It silted down from the river and made the ocean in front of the plantation impossible for swimming. Fine with me. If I wanted to swim, I'd hit one of the beaches nearby. Or swim laps in the pool. I wasn't a good swimmer, but I did a splendid dog paddle.

Sipping my martini, I watched the waves lap the sand. The other dogs joined us but were wary. I was patient, and the dogs were patient with me. They were an odd pack, no fighting among them as if they knew they needed to get along to survive. I understood. We understood each other.

After sunset—no green flash—I walked back to the cottage and found the inner door open. I'd closed it, hadn't I? I had. But I hadn't locked it.

Tempest followed me inside. She sniffed around like she was on the hunt. I followed her to the bedroom. Someone had left a gun on the bedside table.

55

I woke to loud knocking on my door. After a rough night with little sleep, I wanted to use that gun on my visitor. No one ever pounded on my door, especially with the dogs there. Where were the dogs? I checked the bedside clock. Nine a.m.

I was in my undies, so I threw on a beach cover-up and peeked through the blinds. A jogger, maybe in her fifties.

I unlocked the door but kept the screen door between us. "Yes?"

"Hi. My name is Karen." She paused. She was wearing a tracksuit and running shoes. Her brown hair was in a stylish, sporty bob. She was lithe and very tan with good skin. "The manager said you care for a few of the dogs around here? A female with a white, left-front paw?"

I hugged myself. The dogs were gone. I'd let Tempest out last night and now she was nowhere in sight.

"Is she OK?"

"I have her at my cabin. She's bleeding badly from a cut. I applied a tourniquet, but she needs a vet. I was going to take her, but when I heard she stayed at your cabin, I thought you might want to go with me."

I held up a finger, ran into the house, put on some clothes, grabbed my purse, and followed the woman to her cottage where Tempest lay on the porch, panting. She half-heartedly snarled at the woman.

"I'm a nurse," said Karen. "I had to give her a sedative before I could apply the tourniquet."

I wondered how she'd managed that.

Tempest let me pick her up, and we headed for Karen's car.

The vet saved Tempest's leg, but said she might lose some of her motor skills, making her vulnerable. I needed a permanent place to live, and when I did find one, Tempest would go with me.

Back in her car, Karen asked, "You OK?"

My mind was back on the gun and who'd left it.

I snapped, "I'm concerned, that's all."

Karen emitted a sharp, "Oh."

"Sorry. It's bothering me, what the vet said about the cut not being an accident."

Karen nodded. "I wondered about that, too, but didn't want to alarm you."

"The vet said it looked more like someone took a swipe at her with a knife or box cutter." I shuddered. "They couldn't have held her down. She won't let people get that close."

"Islanders don't like strays, especially the aggressive ones."

"Tempest isn't aggressive. She's had a tough life and is leery of people, but she wouldn't attack unless she felt endangered. Or was attacked."

"You don't know that, River."

Reluctantly, I said, "You're right." However, her use of my name irritated me. I'd always had a thing about strangers calling me by name. I wanted a cigarette.

"Thanks for saving Tempest and letting me know."

Karen checked her phone. "Look, I'm hungry. Let's pick up some food from the market and go to the beach. That will help you keep your mind off your dog."

I didn't want to, but Karen had saved Tempest, so I felt obligated. Plus, it had been so long since I'd spent time with a woman. Since Sophie, as a matter of fact. Sophie had always wanted to take a sister trip to Hawaii with me. My heart opened a little.

She said, "We can take a picnic up to Haena State Park. My brother used to live on a commune up there."

"A commune? Do you know this island well?"

"I've been here many times."

"OK," I said. "But I'm buying lunch."

We went to the market, but Karen insisted on picking out the food and wouldn't let me pay. "You relax," she said. "What are friends for?" A shiver went up my spine. Friends? Maybe she was just a caregiver type. She *was* a nurse. But that didn't mean anything. I let it go. We headed for Haena, north of Kapaa, and Kilauea Bay and Lighthouse.

Karen told me about her brother as she sped along the East side of the island.

"Back in the sixties, Elizabeth Taylor's brother, Howard, was denied a permit to build a house on his land, so out of revenge, he bailed thirteen homeless hippies from the Lihue jail and told them they could camp there. They built tree houses out of bamboo, beautiful tree houses. More people came. Surfers and hippies. Dreamers and dropouts. There's even a documentary about Taylor Camp."

I'd always thought that in another time a commune would have attracted Sophie.

Karen looked as if she was going to cry. "My brother found Taylor Camp after he got out of 'Nam. He loved it. Gave him a sense of peace."

"Where's your brother now?"

"Dead. Overdose. But that was much later. He was bipolar."

"So sorry." I felt for her. I'd lost a sister and she'd lost a brother.

By the time we arrived at Hanalei Bay, I was starving and had heard every detail of Taylor Camp. Most of the people living there thought it was paradise. When the commune's children became adults, they had opposing stories of what had happened to them. Some said they'd lived an idyllic life as one big family. Others felt they had no parental supervision, and kids shunned them at school. As her brother had observed, the commune made most of the kids lazy with no idea about life in the bigger world.

I shook my head. "That sounds like almost everyone's take on growing up whether in a commune or not." Karen nodded.

We arrived at Haena State Park and carried a blanket and box lunches down to one of the most beautiful beaches on the island—and that was saying something because almost every beach in Kauai was beautiful.

Karen spread the blanket, and we ate sandwiches as she continued to talk about the island and her brother in almost a stream of consciousness. So far, she'd asked nothing about me. That was OK. Besides what could I say? I'd have to make up a lot of shit.

Then she said, "You had hippy parents, right? That was why I thought you'd be interested in the commune."

At first, I was puzzled, then remembered my alias. "Yes, but my family didn't live in a commune. We lived near a river." I chuckled then redirected the conversation. "Didn't you say you're from Boston? Do you have children?"

She studied me. "I think you're beautiful."

I was not the only one trying to redirect this conversation. "Thanks, but you didn't answer my question."

A breeze blew off the ocean. Up the beach, the Nāpali cliffs careened dangerously into the water.

"No," she said. "No children." She looked over at a family with three kids. We also had that in common. Dead sibling. No kids. I wondered what it would've been like if Hank and I had had children. I felt a stab of empathy for Karen.

She jumped up. "Come on. I'll show you where the commune was."

"If you don't mind, I'd rather relax and enjoy the beach. Besides, that sandwich was filling." I rubbed my belly. Then I noticed her lunch box. She'd barely touched her sandwich.

Karen dropped onto the blanket, slipped on fashion sunglasses, and turned slightly away from me. Then she brushed invisible crumbs from her hands, took out a little brown vial, and snorted something from her long pinkie fingernail. I tried to hide my astonishment. She offered the bottle to me. "No thanks." She looked disappointed. I had no idea what she was snorting. Now I wanted to ask a dozen questions but kept it simple. "What is it?"

"It's pharmaceutical-grade cocaine, my treat on vacations." She exhaled languorously as if in a commercial for the stuff.

"No worries," I said. If only Karen knew what laws *I'd* broken.

She leaned back on her elbows and watched the ocean. I

laid down on my back, an arm over my eyes. Karen rolled over next to me, so close I could smell her breath. "Want to go for a swim?"

I opened my eyes and said, "We just ate." For a nurse, she seemed a little oblivious to healthy habits.

"I'm not making you happy."

Making me *happy*? I sat up. "I'm worried about my dog. And it's not your job to make me happy. I just met you."

"I just thought—"

"I'm sorry. That was rude."

Karen gave me a forced smile. "If you need to talk to someone, I'm here."

"I'd like to go back to the Plantation if you don't mind."

"Are you sure you wouldn't like to see where the commune was? It's so incredibly beautiful."

"Thanks. Maybe some other time." I crushed the to-go box. She was too pushy about seeing the damn commune. If she'd approached me with "I'd like to see it but don't want to go alone," I would have gone, but something about the whole thing felt ... forced.

At the car, Karen screamed. I rushed to the driver's side. "Are you OK?"

She pointed. A hairy orb weaver spider crawled along the door. Probably a female that had dropped from a tree. I brushed it off. Karen shuddered. "I hate spiders." Obviously.

Back at the Plantation, it was a relief to leave Karen and return to my cabin. As soon as I saw the porch and no Tempest, my heart dropped. I patted the other dogs and promised them dinner. Inside, I used the cabin phone to call the vet. Tempest was doing well, but they wanted to keep her a day or two more. They were worried about infection.

"Can I come see her tomorrow?" The vet encouraged this. I said thanks.

Around eight o'clock the next morning, Karen knocked on my door again. "Hey, how's your pooch doing?" She had a box of something in her hands. I didn't let her in, but told her what the vet had said. "Good to play it safe." She lifted the box lid. "I bought some *malasadas* for breakfast."

Donuts. Christ. I felt queasy. I hadn't eaten a donut since after having sex with Sam in Portland.

"You know what these are, right?"

"Yes," I said. "They're known as Hawaiian donuts but are actually Portuguese." My tone was unfriendly.

She was no longer smiling. She looked down as if I'd spit on them.

"I'm sorry, Karen, but I'm busy right now. I can't talk."

Karen closed the box and looked hard at me. "Can I say something?"

I didn't respond.

"I think something pretty traumatic has happened to you. I see symptoms of PTSD and withdrawal, unhealthy signs of being unable to communicate. Plus, I've observed paranoia. You can't be a nurse for as long as I have and turn it all off. Can you tell me if I'm right?"

"Karen, I hardly know you. I'm thankful for what you did for Tempest, but I don't feel comfortable talking with you about my personal life."

Karen exhaled noisily through her teeth and squinted. Something other than exasperation glinted in her eyes. Hate. But why hate? I probably *was* paranoid.

"Look, Karen, I appreciate your concern. I do. But I'm fine." I wanted her to leave.

"OK. Thanks for letting me say that. I can be a little over-protective." She paused.

I waited, foot tapping.

"I won't ask any more questions. I leave on Friday and

would like to hike Waimea Canyon. I think some physical exercise would do us both good. How about it? Want to go?"

I was at the point of surrender. Maybe I wasn't physically or mentally healthy. I'd been through a lot, more than most, even more than some criminals I'd prosecuted. She waited patiently for my answer, now a sad, yet hopeful look on her face.

"All right." I didn't want to hike the Canyon. I had a fear of heights, but at this point I'd say anything to get rid of her.

Suddenly, she was smiling and cheery. "It's beautiful! Wait until you see the coastline from up high. This island is like a magic carpet. It will help you mend."

Mend? As she walked down the steps toward the black sand, I wondered if I'd regret this.

56

That night, I had another nightmare and woke, drenched with sweat. This one left me shaking as if I'd stepped on a live wire. Disjointed images of a hanging body in blue that turned out to be Hank. Sophie's body washed up at our feet while Karen and I ate lunch. Someone picked the lock on my front door and hummed "Tainted Love," Sophie's favorite song, so I pulled out the gun and fired. I didn't need a shrink to tell me who my ghosts were.

It was three a.m. A warm shower relaxed me. I wrapped in a blanket and fell asleep in a chair. Around eight o'clock, the pounding rain of a tropical storm woke me. My first thought was for Tempest, *my* dog. She shook during storms. She'd be scared at the vet hospital.

After throwing on clothes and a rain jacket, I gathered the old beach towel she slept on, some treats, and headed to the animal hospital. The on-duty med tech took me back where I sat on the floor in front of Tempest's open cage and scratched her ears. The med tech suspected former abuse as there were signs of old injuries. I wanted to cry. Loud voices from the waiting room drew my attention.

Karen rushed in, dripping wet, wide-eyed, followed by the admittance person. "Oh, God, I was so worried about you, River. I thought Tempest had died."

I jumped to my feet. What the fuck?

"Ma'am," the tech said to Karen, "would you please have a seat in the waiting room." The tech's tone was soft yet stern.

I took Karen's arm, led her into the bathroom, and closed the door. "What the hell is *wrong* with you?"

"I was running early this morning—I'm an insomniac—and saw your lights on."

You're a lot more than an insomniac, lady.

"Then later I noticed your car was gone. All I could think of is something had happened to your dog."

"To my dog? Why?"

She didn't answer.

I didn't like this. Not one bit. Why would anyone run in a tropical storm?

Her rain jacket dripped on the floor. I still had hold of her arm. She was so sinewy I could touch my finger to my thumb around her arm. Insomnia, the skinniness, the skitzy behavior—she was a druggie. How many addicted dealers had I helped prosecute for God's sake?

"Look," I said, trying to keep a neutral tone. "I appreciate your concern, but you're overreacting to everything. Maybe you need to talk with someone, a professional I mean."

She plopped onto the toilet, covered her face with her hands, and sobbed.

Jesus.

"Karen, what's going on?" I tried to sound compassionate, but I didn't need this.

"I'm ... sorry." She choked on her words. "I'm supposed to be taking antidepressants, but I stopped. I didn't tell you. I lost my husband a while back. I'm pretty raw."

I unrolled some toilet paper and handed it to her. "I'm sorry."

"This is where we honeymooned ... on Kauai." She stood up and blew her nose. "You're right. I am overreacting."

I took a deep breath. "Why don't you go home and take a nap. Or when the rain stops, go for a run?"

She sniffled. "I thought we were going on a hike."

Shit. I was not in the mood. "It's too wet. Another day, OK?"

She looked at the floor where rainwater dripped from her raincoat. "I've made a mess."

"Go home, Karen. It's fine. It's only water."

Despite my better instincts, I'd let someone—and of all people, *this* woman—get too close. Her emotional neediness was more than I could handle.

I watched her drive away, sighed with relief, and turned to the vet tech. "Can I please take Tempest home?"

"If you insist, but tomorrow would be best," she said.

On my way to the car, I wondered who Karen was. Did I even know her last name? Wait. She had told me. Carmichael. From Boston. Now I had some research to do. Maybe she was just a druggie, but I thought she was something else. Could she be the person the dogs had chased down the beach and into the shadows? No. That person had been tall.

Then again, was I overreacting? Maybe she was irrational because of her loss. People in grief were like that sometimes. Still, I'd check her background. Back in the day, I'd been damn good at sniffing out other's intention and ulterior motives. I'd made sure I had all the evidence, even doing research on my own time and following leads the cops either ignored or missed. It had often paid off. I also watched for possible personality disorders, like bipolar, borderline, sociopath, or psychopath. (Hank had used to say I should have been a forensic psychologist.) Never had dismissed any possibility, especially when dealing with criminals.

In the parking lot, I leaned against my car. I craved a cigarette. The rain had stopped, and the air was fresh. I reminded myself that Karen would leave in a few days. But I couldn't squelch my curiosity. I needed to know who she was. Her interest in me was abnormal. Was she stalking me?

Then a crazy thought hit—could Karen be connected to Steve? I'd never felt Steve was telling the truth. Plus, he wouldn't leave me alone. But why would he engage or employ someone like Karen? Was Karen's "crazy" an act? Sam's sweet, romantic nature had been an act. Who the hell was Steve? Who the hell was Karen? God!

Now that I'd been off my meds for a month, my brain was firing at top speed. I needed to contact Snoop to see if she'd ever found out anything about Steve. A connection between him and my former law firm, or with Sam? But my burner phone didn't do SnapChat, so I'd have to call her—if she'd answer my "unknown" number.

I thought about the many times my sister and I had chatted on the phone, the number of times I'd called Hank. Hank and I had talked more on the phone than we ever had at home, what with my job and his traveling. My chest ached with missing him. He knew me so well. We knew each other.

Ha. That was such bullshit. I hadn't known Hank. I'd never thought he'd cheat on me, especially with my sister. So if I couldn't trust him or her, who could I trust? No one.

57

I was fired up when I reached the Plantation. I was also hungry.

As I headed to my cottage, the dogs growled but not at me.

When I reached the porch, I froze. Steve sat in one of the cane chairs, cool as could be, patting one of the dogs. Sweat broke out on my upper lip and under my arms. My instinct was to run, but I pulled it together and walked up the stairs. How dare he make himself at home. I could have smacked the shit out of him.

I approached him. "What the hell are you doing here?"

He looked up as if he had just seen me. "I like your new spiky red hair. It brings out your cheekbones."

"Fuck you. What are you doing here?"

He smiled down at the dog he was patting. "Looking for you," he said, all relaxed, as if we were good friends.

"Why?"

"Because you disappeared, and we were worried. Thought you might have been a victim of the scumbags we're trying to catch."

He had dressed in full Hawaiian gear—Local's brand sandals, cotton shirt, cutoff jeans, sunglasses on his head. He was holding the only personal item I'd brought from San Francisco, my copy of *Power*. He was in my cottage. I looked over at the door. Of course he'd been in there. He'd been in it before. He'd left the gun. But why? And should I ask him? My gut said *no*.

"What do you want?"

"Another date."

"Look, asshole. What. Do. You. Want? And what do you mean when you said *we* were worried?"

"OK." He stood. I looked up. His demeanor now had a military edge. His voice was clipped. "Let's talk inside."

"No."

I crossed my arms and continued to hold eye contact as my insides painfully crimped. He could tell I wouldn't obey his orders.

Finally, he said, "Did you know Sam Donleavy, aka Carl Wood?"

I was so surprised by this I laughed. "Really? You came all the way here to ask me that?" Then I realized my mistake. "And exactly how would I know this Sam, aka Carl?"

"The night after our date, you had a date with him at the Hotel deLuxe."

"Who do you work for? Show me ID." I held out my hand.

He took a wallet badge from his back pocket, opened it for me to see, but wouldn't hand it over. The blue FBI logo was writ large across the top.

His name was William Augustus Martin. Special Agent.

I knew from experience IDs could be faked. If he were FBI, I was in a world of hurt. If he was working for someone else, I was in a world of hurt.

"You can call me Gus."

I said, "Tell me what's going on."

"You first. Tell me about your date with Sam."

"Really?"

He nodded.

"The guy bought me a delicious romantic meal then he fucked me like a porn star."

Steve-Gus flinched. Ha! He'd remembered our fumbling, drunken failure at sex. He quickly recovered. "Is that why you were meeting him again in Eugene at the Fifth Street Market, to have sex? Was that it, Ang?"

So he knew my real name. I countered with, "Is that why you were stalking me, Augustus?" He didn't answer. "Is Sam wanted for something?"

"He's dead."

I faked surprise, attempted to say something, couldn't.

"Why did you meet him at the Multnomah Whiskey Library?"

Shit. Steve-Gus knew. What else did he know? If he were FBI, he could have phone records. He'd know I called Sam.

"We had a drink. I said no to Sam's advances, told him I didn't want to ruin a perfect memory. Outside, he kissed me, and I went back to the hotel."

"The Crystal." He watched me as if he knew everything and was waiting for me to confess. Then he said, "What was the fight about?"

"What fight?"

"The fight you had when he was holding you against his car."

"That wasn't a fight. Jesus. He was pushy, wanted sex, and I had to get a little forceful with the *no*."

"Was he blackmailing you?"

I snorted. "Look, Gus, this would be a lot easier if you

told me what you're after?" I could smell cigarette on him. I needed one bad. "Do you have a smoke?"

He pulled a pack from a shirt pocket, lit one for me and one for him, and said, "This would be a lot more comfortable if we sat down." He was back to the casual Aloha islander.

We sat and smoked for a bit before he said, "Why'd you change your identity?"

I was surprised when I heard myself say, "Because I lost everything."

"What do you mean?"

"I lost my sister, my law career, my husband. Nothing seemed to be going right. I'd always had to manage my sister. She made lousy choices. I loved Hank and couldn't imagine loving anyone else. When I lost my position then law license, I had nothing. Just some money. I was looking at a long legal battle for Hank's business, and I was tired. I just wanted to leave it all behind."

So much of this was true, my eyes stung. I snuffled back tears.

"Even what you'd receive when they settle your husband's business affairs?"

"You and I both know those battles can rage on, and I could end up with nothing."

"Did you poison Sam?"

I looked him in the eye. "Is that how he died?"

"Why'd you leave the Crystal so soon? You running from something?"

Saying everything out loud had cracked something in me. I truly had lost everything.

"Ang?"

My voice broke as I said, "I left because I was afraid he'd come to the hotel. He seemed obsessed with me. I just couldn't deal with it. Worrying if he'd knock on my door. First, you were texting me, then driving by my house. Yes, I saw you. Then him tracking me down." I paused. "So he's dead? You're not making that up?"

"He's dead. And you're the last person to see him alive."

"No. The person who poisoned him is the last one to see him alive."

"I forget I'm dealing with a former attorney." He stabbed out a half-finished cig on the railing then folded a piece of gum into his mouth. When we made eye contact, he said, "On the night you and I were at the Hotel Vintage, why did you say you killed someone?"

I was puzzled. And now scared. "I didn't say that."

"Yes, you did. I have a recording of it."

"You recorded us? For fuck's sake, Steve, I mean Gus. Isn't it against the law to record without my consent? And why *would* you record us?"

He chewed like a trucker on speed. His eyes were black hubcaps. "Look, Ang, I know about the dates and the blackmail."

Bile rose in my throat. I wondered if he'd come to take me in. Maybe this was it.

"But we aren't after you. You're small fry."

"Thanks a lot," I said with a half laugh. "And who says *small fry* anymore?" He smiled and snapped his gum.

Gus could be lying. For some reason, I didn't think so. I stared out at the ocean. It was dark and still. The air smelled like rotting fish. The dogs hung around me, their hackles quivering. I glanced back at Gus. He leaned forward.

"We *were* after this guy Sam-Carl-David-whatever. He and his operation extort millions out of women. He was one of your dates. So we thought you'd know something about him."

Where was he going with this? I needed to stay naive. "He even bought me a present."

"You mean the beetle in the glass box?"

My chest pinched. "You *know* about that?"

"It was his shtick. He pretended to be a coleopterist figuring not many women wanted to know about his career studying bugs. I don't know how many times he tried to give that 'gift' to one of his marks."

I rubbed the back of my neck. So stupid, but I felt a little cheated. As Gus chewed, I thought about the word *gumshoe*. Stupid thought.

"Can you tell me anything about Sam?" he asked.

At this point, what did I have to lose? What did I know that would be important? "He said he founded a non-profit veterinarian service to aid the animals of the homeless."

"Another one of his shticks. Women love it."

"So it's not true. Sam said his wife was a Lesbian."

"His wife is bi-sexual."

"Really?"

"Cross my heart," and he did. I hadn't seen anyone do that since I was a kid.

"Why would he do that?"

"He married Betty Snayer because she's wealthy. I'm guessing she married him because he was 'sweet and charming,' a regular narcissist. We're pretty sure she funded his operation, maybe even heads it." Gus paused. "Why'd he leave early that night?"

"What? Oh, you mean the night I was with him?" I felt lightheaded. "He had an emergency call from home. Their arrangement—if she calls, he has to go."

"Any idea why?"

"All he said was his wife needed him. He didn't explain."

"So you didn't get any money out of him."

"Was Sam the leader of this extortion racket?"

"You mean Lincoln Stillwater the Third?"

"What?"

"His real name."

"No!"

"I kid you not. His nickname was 'Link.'"

"Lincoln 'Link' Stillwater the Third?"

We laughed.

I finished my cigarette and stubbed it out. "How much damage has he done?"

"He had, or still has, global operatives working. He's ripped off around one hundred and seventy-five million—that we know of."

I wondered when he was going to tell me he knew about Gerard and Sophie. He seemed to know about everything else. I waited. I started to itch and sweat. The past was sitting on my front porch. And he wasn't done with me yet.

"Are you going to prosecute me?"

Gus shook his head.

I stared at him until he met my eyes. "Can you make a promise like that?"

"If the Bureau doesn't know about you—and they don't, yet—your little Ashley Madison gig disappears."

Between stress and relief at this news, my body turned cold and shaky. My stomach heaved. I ran to the bathroom where I sat on the toilet lid, dizzy, head in hands. A gecko scurried past.

When the dizziness passed, I realized I hadn't eaten and grabbed a handful of crackers from the kitchen. I had no idea why Gus was here if not to arrest me.

Back on the porch, Gus was gone.

58

Steve-Gus had done it again—made me edgy, the rat bastard. I needed info. Like now. Inside, I locked the door, took out my burner, held my breath, and called Snoop.

"I'm sorry. The number you are calling is no longer in service. You may—"

I disconnected. Shit. Now what? I couldn't chance using a library computer. At the fridge, I ate leftover rice, drank coconut milk from the container. It wasn't hot today, but I was sweating.

My brain raced. If Gus knew where I was, maybe one of Sam's partners did too. If Gus suspected me of killing Sam, so would one of Sam's partners. I hated this cat and mouse game Gus was playing with me. He was probably hoping to scare a confession out of me. He could threaten to take me in for killing Sam, but all the evidence was circumstantial. So far.

I wished there were a way—

My burner phone rang. I stared at it like it was a terrorist bomb. It could be Gus. I could hardly swallow. When I picked it up, I took a deep breath and answered.

A distorted voice said, "You just called me. Tell me something that only we know."

I flopped on the couch in relief. It was Snoop. Had to be. I said, "Ashley Madison. Gerard Duvernet. Steve."

I waited, but nothing happened. I was about to hang up when I heard, "This is Snoop. Hi, Ang." The voice was now clear.

"Snoop!" What relief. "Thanks for calling back." Funny, but I still couldn't tell if Snoop was male or female by the voice, but I was so glad to hear from her—or him.

She wasted no time on chitchat. "I've looked into that French guy, Gerard Duvernet. Are you sure this guy's dead?"

"What? Why?"

"The living can disappear, but the dead seldom do. How do you know this guy's dead?"

"Because I poisoned him."

I heard an intake of breath. I didn't think anything could surprise Snoop.

"O ... K. ..." Snoop said. "I can't find anything on him—no obit, no mortuary, no announcement in any paper or online."

"So that means he could be at the bottom of the ocean wrapped in concrete."

"I found nothing through his government job. Are you sure he worked for them?"

I hugged a pillow. "I'm not sure of anything."

"If someone dropped him in the middle of the ocean, there would be a missing persons report. Like the one on you. I even checked the cell number you gave me. There's no record of a Gerard Duvernet with that number."

Silence.

"How much do you know about this guy?"

I told her the whole story. Then I waited.

Finally, she said, "If he turned informant, he might have changed his identity. If the partner is dead, he could come out of hiding, but others might want to ax him."

"I'm pretty sure I killed him." Then again, was I?

"If you did, some government agency or some organization covered it up."

"Shit. I don't know where to go with that."

I was done, but she said, "That other guy, Steve? His name is Augustus, and he's FBI. He might've used the Ashley Madison site to go after the ring because they use it."

"Yes, I know. He showed up on my front porch today and showed me ID. I wonder how he found me? I have no GPS, changed my ID, and appearance."

"No clue. Maybe the old-fashioned way—he tailed you," Snoop said.

"What about facial recognition?"

"Nope. Video cam footage sucks. The national system isn't sophisticated enough yet." A phone rang at her end. It stopped. She asked, "Could he be tracking someone else who is tracking you?"

My heart beat like a hovering helicopter. "Snoop, you said there's a missing persons report on me? Do you know who filed it?"

"Your attorney."

My throat constricted. I didn't know why this got to me. If I had disappeared, someone would have gotten my share of Hank's business. I knew that from the beginning. But hearing I was a "missing person?" Kind of like being told I'm dead. I startled when Snoop said, "You there?"

"Yes," I breathed out. "I might have more work for you. First, I want to do a little snooping myself." A slight snuffle of laughter. Good. Snoop had a sense of humor. "You now have my burner number. It's a stripped down version. No internet or text."

"Gotcha. But you need to trash it and get another one. Regularly."

I said OK, and we hung up. I took the gun from my dresser drawer, made sure it was loaded, laid it on the kitchen counter, and planned my next move.

59

Gus would return. I was sure of that. But until then, I'd be watching Karen. My brain went on the hunt. She showed up when Tempest was hurt. Tempest's slash hadn't been accidental. Had Karen done that to meet me, to make a connection? The trip to the Haena beach would not have raised alarms except, with my paranoia, she felt pushy about hiking into her brother's old commune. Then there'd been the scene at the animal hospital. All too forced. However, I reminded myself that the woman used coke, so all of her behavior could be drug-related.

I found my old half pack of cigarettes and lit one. It was a little stale. With the gun stuffed down the back of my jeans and the bottom of my hoodie pulled over it, I felt like a criminal on a television show. On the beach, I paced and smoked.

Karen said she lost her husband recently. I shivered. What if she *was* Sam's wife? What if she was out for revenge? But how could she have possibly found me? A smooth move on her part to act crazy. She knew it could either distract me or make me underestimate her. Did she want to kill me? Easy to do if I'd gone with her to see the commune property. Maybe she wanted to hike the canyon so she could shove me over the edge. She didn't look like a killer, but I'd once had a client who looked, acted, and talked like a grandmotherly librarian. She killed a couple who poisoned her cats. You never knew.

The wind came up and flicked ash into my eye. I crushed the cigarette in the sand and stuck the filter in my pocket. It was too late to hit a library computer to look for photos of Betty Snayer.

Screw it. I wouldn't wait for the next move. I'd make my own. I'd take Karen to dinner.

Back at the cottage, I slipped on a yellow cotton shift, my wedge sandals, and dangling shell earrings. A touch of lip gloss, my sunglasses, and I was ready. I flung my bag over my shoulder, slid the gun into the outside pocket, and headed to Karen's.

60

The next morning, I dressed, made my first cup of coffee of the day, and fed the pack. Last night was a bust. At the Grand Hyatt Tidepools, Karen drank a martini, two glasses of wine and an aperitif, yet remained sharp enough to avoid my questions. She ate very little of her tofu dish. Probably on visits to the ladies' room, she snorted a line or two.

So much for me making a move.

Now I didn't know what to do about her. She was one tough nut. She'd avoided anything that opened the safety deposit box of her life, making me even more suspicious. But a few details had emerged. She lived in a townhouse in Boston and collected naïve art. A nurse's salary wouldn't support that. She also found it distasteful to take home leftovers. When I'd asked for a to-go box for the remains of my Mahi dish and the dessert *she* ordered but didn't eat, she wrinkled her nose as if this wasn't *de rigueur*. So she was snooty which reeked of old money, or maybe aspirations for old money.

Hungry, I pulled the coconut chiffon mousse cake from

my fridge and wolfed it down with my coffee. My chest bubbled with memories of sharing a piece of Sophie's favorite coconut cream pie with her. She'd usually come over to tell me about her latest guy. Coffee, pie—and me trying *not* to point out the guy's troublesome behavior. Now I wished I had. Now I wished I'd pointed out *her* troublesome behavior—like choosing the same kind of guy over and over.

With notebook in my shoulder bag, I rechecked the safety on the gun and grabbed the car keys to head to the library where I'd research the hell out of Karen.

Suddenly, the phone rang. It was the veterinary hospital. I could take Tempest home.

I glanced at the clock. It was eight-thirty.

"I'll be there right after I hit the library."

"But the library's closed until noon."

Right. It was Wednesday. Damn.

Back home with Tempest, I found a note from Karen taped to my front door. "I'm ready to go anytime. Come on over!"

The canyon hike.

Why go? Why invite danger? But there was little privacy in the canyon. Too many tourists. It wasn't like she could push me off or pretend that I'd jumped. I hated heights. Wouldn't get close enough to the edge for her to do me in. I had a gun, and I wasn't afraid to use it. Maybe I'd get some info out of her. I needed to know who she was and what she wanted.

I changed my clothes, packed my daypack with ID, wallet, water, and sunscreen, and slipped the gun into the inside pocket of my jacket, something I'd wear even though it was warm. Tempest planted herself at the front door, and I walked over to Karen's—if that was her name.

61

We were in the backseat of Karen's car. A guy named Mike was driving. He had a buzz cut, a square head, and massive shoulders that dwarfed the steering wheel. From what I could see of his face, he was expressionless and reminded me of a movie hitman.

Karen explained that, since her husband had died, Mike traveled with her on vacation as security.

My inner alarm level was orange. "How come I haven't seen him until now?" I was pissed. I could only see the back of Mike's head and grabbed at the headrest of driver's seat. He didn't flinch. Only the rich, the celebrities, and politicians traveled with body guards.

Karen wouldn't look at me. "I'm sorry. I should have told you about him earlier."

"Why do you need security? Are you in danger? Are *we* in danger?"

"No, no. We're perfectly safe. I wanted Mike to drive today so he could drop us off and pick us up. Parking sucks at the lookouts."

"Again, why haven't I seen him until now?"

"Every *other* time, I've been with *you* and didn't need him." Her defensive tone made me feel for the gun. Karen had a motive for dragging me up here, and it wasn't to see the canyon.

Then she leaned in, touched my arm, and said, "River, thanks for going today." Her teary eyes blinked as we climbed Route 505 on the way to the Waimea Canyon trails. "This is the last thing my husband and I did on our honeymoon."

This woman changed signals like a traffic light. Now she was all mushy, going into detail about what they'd done on their honeymoon, how romantic he'd been. Giving her a gift every day. Swimming together at midnight under a full moon. Watching whales fight over a female at Poipu. Kissing at visits to an albatross preserve, the Kilauea Lighthouse, and Shipwreck Beach.

I didn't buy it. Karen's stories sounded more like Hallmark movie scenarios. Hank could be romantic, but he'd never lapsed into this kind of sentimentality. I didn't trust anything she said. I looked out the window and wondered how I could escape if the day turned ugly. I had to bolt. I missed Hank and what we could have had. I wished Sophie and I could have come here.

Karen kept talking, but I'd missed half of what she said. "He loved the canyon and could tell you everything about it. It's ten miles long, a mile wide, and more than 3,500 feet deep. Hopefully, it's clear up here today so you can see the Pacific Ocean, plus the island of Ni'ihau. No one is allowed on the—"

I knew most of this, but I didn't let on. Mike pulled off at one of the trailheads, dropped us off, and drove away. We shouldered our packs and walked a hundred yards to the overlook where tourists aimed their cameras at the canyon, took selfies, and yelled at children to stand back from the guardrails. Thick clouds crowned the upper reaches of the canyon, but below, the three-thousand-foot drop gave me a tremor. I stepped back.

Karen said, "You just turned pale. Don't like heights?"

A sweat broke out on my forehead.

Suddenly, Karen jumped the guardrail. A woman screamed and grabbed her child. Karen stood on the ledge, looking down. A man shouted, "Stop her!" as if she was going to leap. I knew better.

"What the fuck, Karen!"

She turned, smiled, and jumped back over the guardrail as effortlessly as a gymnast. The crowd quickly moved away. I was shaking.

"What in hell was *that*?" I wanted to *throw* her into the canyon.

"I did that when I was with my husband. He was upset like you are, but I told him life is full of risks, and fear is debilitating." There was a flush to her cheeks and a smile that would have been magnetic if not for what I'd just witnessed.

I glowered at her. A mother nearby embraced her scared daughter. The daughter, blonde with rosy cheeks, reminded me of Sophie at that age. Between my teeth, I said, "Yeah? Well, there's a thing called common sense. Plus, you just scared that little girl over there."

Karen snorted. "You sound just like my mother."

No doubt. I'd bet even Karen's mother thought she was a little mental. This jumping the guardrail put me on edge. Karen was probably counting on that for a reason. You'd think if she wanted to do me harm, she'd try to put me at ease.

"Come on," she said and headed toward the trail. I thought about turning around, but I needed to see this through. I walked behind her, no conversation for forty minutes. Every so often, I glanced behind me to see if Mike was following us, but I didn't see him. When we reached the vantage point overlooking the canyon, I was a little breathless even though it was an easy hike. I started sweating when I saw there were no guardrails.

Karen walked the perimeter. One guy was on his belly and had snaked up to the edge to see over. Not to be outdone, Karen did the same.

I stood a good twenty feet back. The clouds shifted, lighting up the canyon in layers of green, brown and bright rust. Beyond the canyon, the ocean brimmed deep blue.

When people joined us, I relaxed. She couldn't push me off in front of witnesses. But I didn't go close enough for that to happen anyway.

When Karen joined me, she was oblivious to the stares of people who had watched her jump the guardrail. I was done with her dramatics. Fuck this.

"I'm heading back to the car. Beautiful view, but too high up for me." I turned and walked away. Karen hesitated then hurried to join me. As if an afterthought, I stopped and said, "I forgot. What was your husband's name?"

"Lincoln, but everyone called him Link."

Stunned, I moved to the side of the trail. Jesus. When I turned to face her, what I saw was unmistakable—she knew who I was and what that meant.

She seemed unfazed. In almost a whisper, she said, "I wish you'd chill. You're in no danger. You did me a favor killing Link."

I glanced down the trail. No Mike in sight. "Link? Who the hell it that?"

"He often went by Sam. Sometimes Carl."

I took a deep breath. "How'd you find me?"

"Mike's been following you. In Portland, he almost missed you when you left the Crystal. Then in San Francisco, you almost gave him the slip. Let's go back to the Plantation. I'll make us some drinks and explain everything. You're in no danger from me."

She started walking again. I wondered what she meant about being in no danger from her. Was I in danger from someone else? When we reached the lookout and parking lot, she called Mike to pick us up.

"So you're Betty Snayer," I said. She nodded. "In that case, I'll get a different ride back."

She touched my arm. "Please. You need to believe me. You *did* do me a favor. Link was out of control. I was scared of him."

Mike pulled up before I could ask what she meant by doing her a favor. She obviously was convinced I had killed him. But I'd had plenty of experience with cops and other lawyers who used the same tactic of "shock and awe" to catch someone off guard and force a confession or say something damning.

She said, "Mike saw what happened. In the car. Pretty impressive. Link would have killed you, you know."

Funny about what crossed my mind when nailed for murder. *How did a big guy like Mike stay in the shadows? How could he witness something like me poisoning Sam when it was night, and the car had tinted windows? How could he be sure of what I was doing?*

I stayed quiet.

"Come on," she said. "Let's get in. I'm dying for a smoke."

We climbed into the back. From a pack, Karen--now Betty--tapped out two cigarettes, lit one, and handed it to me. I took a deep drag and exhaled a long plume of satisfying smoke. Mike pulled onto the road.

My brain processed all Gus had told me and what I now knew. Gus wasn't after me. I was just a lucky find. He was after Betty.

"I owe you," she said. "I married Link on the rebound after my long-time girlfriend had an affair with some debutante." She sighed. "With Link, I fell for all the wrong traits. Men. Christ. We met in a bar. He bought me a drink and told me about his girlfriend who had left him for a Silicon Valley hotshot. I could relate. Of course, it was all lies."

She waited for me to say something. I smoked and asked Mike to lower my window a few inches.

"Link and I got along. He didn't have to worry about money. I enjoyed him because he was fun and romantic—at first. But he gambled, and when I told him he couldn't gamble anymore with my money, he turned nasty. That was right around the time I heard Madoff ripped off many of my Jewish friends. I had no patience with Link crying about not being able to gamble. Then he presented me with his crazy idea."

"Robbing people of their wealth? Like Madoff?" I couldn't hide a smirk.

She turned in the seat towards me. "No. Going after Wall Street traders, land grabbers, corrupt CEOs, and wealthy assholes who buy corrupt politicians." She swallowed hard. "He said we'd anonymously give the money to those who've been ripped off. I'd be in charge of that part of the operation."

"What happened to your little Robin Hood scheme?"

"Link told me some story about his father losing his business because of greedy assholes like these guys. He told me his strategy, I financed it, and then last year I found out he was stealing from *anyone* with money, even the honest business people, and coercing vulnerable relatives to steal the money, so he wasn't directly involved. Like he did with your sister." She flicked ash into the car's ashtray. "He had one of his partners seduce her, then steal from your husband's business. He was clever. He somehow forced the victims to keep their mouths shut. He put that money into an untouchable account somewhere."

I stiffened. "So you knew that Link targeted my sister?"

"I'm sorry. Link told me one of his men, a Frenchman named Gerard, went rogue. Said the guy hid the money then disappeared. By then I knew Link was a pathological liar."

I took a deep drag. My heart pounded, and I felt sick thinking of Gerard. I'd dreamed about him the first week I was here after I'd fallen asleep on the beach. In the dream, we made love. I forced myself awake and cried. I wished I'd never gone to Paris. I wished I'd never met him. But my rational side knew it was only physical, nothing but a fantasy about a handsome man. Plus, I was lonely. I missed Hank.

We reached the main road. Karen seemed to be somewhere far away. I recognized that expression, the pain beneath the skin, the desire to set the clock back, to change the choices you'd made, to make everything all right again. But maybe I was projecting *my* feelings onto her. I had to be careful. Her behavior could be a sticky vat of manipulation.

We remained silent until we reach the Plantation. I followed her into her cottage, and she poured two shots of tequila. We drank. No clinking glasses.

I asked, "Why'd you follow me to Kauai?"

She poured two more shots then pulled a gun from her backpack and laid it on the counter.

62

I tossed back the tequila to hide my surprise at the gun. Was Betty trying to scare me? At least it wasn't pointed at me. Maybe she wanted me to know she could have killed me at any time.

"Let's go for a walk on the beach." She grabbed the tequila bottle and walked out, leaving the gun on the counter. I followed. We headed in the direction of my cottage.

The way I felt about her?

Guilty until proven innocent.

The ocean's reflected light cast a surreal glimmer. No shadows showed on the black sand. I shuddered.

Betty kicked off her sandals and chuckled.

"What's so funny?"

"It's a strange world that brings us together like this, don't you think?"

I wasn't telling her what I was thinking.

This woman, at the minimum, financed Link's operation that resulted in my sister's death and me losing Hank.

Betty sipped from the bottle. I'd never seen anyone sip tequila.

"I have a proposition for you," she said as she handed me the bottle. "I'm taking over this 'Robin Hood scheme' as you call it. First I'm going to do a Superfund cleanup, get rid of the toxic elements."

I wondered if Mike would take care of that.

Karen stopped walking, turned to the ocean, and inhaled with vigor. "Ocean air can clear the head." She glanced over at me. "Ang, I need a woman like you with a sharp intellect and law background. I'd pay you well. Much better than what your firm paid you. I'd treat you with respect."

"Thanks, but I'm not interested. I'm just starting to have a normal life."

She turned to face me. "What the fuck is *normal*, Ang?" She was spitting out the words and gesticulating like mad. "Is any of what's going on in the world normal? Is anything you've been through *normal*?"

I stepped back. "If I worked for you, and you continued to rip people off with the toxic elements, I'd be kind of stuck now, wouldn't I?"

As quickly as she was to anger, Karen was now composed. She studied my face, tried to smile, but couldn't quite pull it off. The less I said, the better. I waited. Finally, she said, "What happened to the Frenchman?"

"What?"

"Gerard was your sister's lover."

"How would I know?"

"Really?" She stepped toward me. "Come on, Ang. Let's be honest with each other. Gerard who had access to the money? Suddenly he disappears and doesn't tell your sister?

So she's heartbroken and hangs herself? Link said they planned to disappear together."

I handed back the bottle. "Link would say anything to save his ass. My sister hanged herself because of Link *and* Gerard. I'm done here. Good night, Betty."

I wanted to run to my cottage, but I didn't. Hank would have said, "Show no fear."

OK. Will do.

He also would have said, "You've got this."

That was questionable.

The pack greeted me, tails wagging. Tempest followed me inside. I locked the door, but this time I shoved a chair under the doorknob.

Sipping three fingers of whiskey I paced, knowing something she'd said had given her away. What the hell was it? I reran the conversation.

Why did she think I would know anything about Gerard? She obviously didn't know what happened to him. If Snoop couldn't find him, neither could Betty. And why would she even care?

Unless.

Two reasons.

Number one—money. Not just the money in Sophie's account. Gerard could have had another account. Betty didn't know Gerard was dead. She thought he'd run off with the money he and Link stashed and wanted to know where it was and how to get it.

Number two—if Gerard were alive, he'd be a threat. Maybe Betty believed he'd been in protective custody, and given up names, evidence of the operation, and the money.

That night I fell asleep in my clothes with Tempest next to my chair and the loaded gun on the side table. An early morning nightmare had me running down the beach and toward the river where I waded into the water. The current carried me out to the ocean, and I went under. I forced myself awake, then doubled up, sputtering and choking.

63

Morning crawled dark and stormy. Rain pelted the deck and side windows. I sat at the kitchen counter, slugging down my first cup of coffee. Tempest sat at my feet, a deep rumble in her throat. The gun was nearby. I didn't know if Tempest was nervous from the storm or if she detected something outside. Karen should be leaving, but I wouldn't be relieved until I knew her cabin was empty.

The chair remained shoved under the door handle. I peeked out the front window. The pack was gone, but that wasn't unusual. During a storm, the dogs often hid.

I called Snoop. She was my only connection to the world, to a feeling of having someone who was watching my back.

A recording again. "The number you have reached is no longer in service." I hung up and waited for her to call back, and then Tempest growled and bared her teeth. She wasn't trembling, so it wasn't thunder.

A knock sounded on the door. My heart jumped.

Tempest snarled. I picked up my gun and shoved it in my hoodie pocket.

A man's voice. "Hello, Ms. Atwood? It's Ted, the manager."

Relieved, I pulled the chair away and opened the door, leaving the screen door between us. Ted was dripping wet. He was also frowning.

"You know the rules. No dogs in the cottages. They give us a terrible flea problem when inside."

"Tempest was injured and has been treated for fleas. I'll take her with me when I find a place to rent."

It didn't matter. Ted wanted the dog out of the cottage. He stepped back and waited. From the bedroom, I grabbed Tempest's blanket and settled her on the porch.

As Ted turned to leave, I asked, "Excuse me, but can you tell me if Karen Carmichael checked out?"

"Yes, she had an early flight." Then he was gone.

I locked the door and leaned back against it, relieved. I could smell my sweat. After a quick shower and change of clothes, I tried to read yesterday's paper, but couldn't concentrate. Snoop still hadn't called back.

I called her again. This time I got a fast busy. Same ten minutes later. Even though I was relieved that Karen was gone, my nerves still twinged. Since she hadn't got what she wanted from me, she could pull a fast one and stay on the island.

I slipped on my raincoat, moved the gun to the coat pocket, and opened the door, expecting Tempest, but she was gone. Instead, Gus walked up the steps.

"Where's your dog pack?" he asked as he approached.

The wind blew violently and pushed Gus forward. I stepped back.

"What are you doing here?"

"I need to come in."

"No, you don't."

"Betty Snayer did not leave the island."

"Shit." I reluctantly opened the screen door.

Inside, I stood at the island counter opposite Gus. I wondered how many women had used kitchen islands as a defense.

"What's going on?" I asked.

"We have a task force ready to arrest Betty as soon as she enters her house in Boston."

"Why wait? Why not arrest her here?"

"We need to have everything in place to convict. We need to arrest Snayer at home and take her computers."

"So? What's that got to do with me?"

"We need you to testify."

I laughed. "The defense would shred me for breaking the law, changing my identity, losing my license, and so forth."

"I have you covered," he said. "The gun I left you? It has a sophisticated microphone in the handle. I have your conversations on record. You helped me nail this outfit."

I tried to read his face. He wasn't kidding. Shit.

"You're fine. You never admitted to killing Link. Plus, her goon couldn't have seen you do it. The car windows were tinted, and other people passed that car all night long. The cops didn't find his body until morning."

"Did you bug Betty's cottage?"

"Yes. That's why she took you to the beach. She's no fool."

I pulled up a stool and stared at Gus. Memories returned of strategies from pre-trial meetings. I drummed my fingers on the counter in hopes it gave the appearance of being nervous but also knowing it rattled opposing council.

Gus finally said, "We also busted the outfit where you bought your fake ID and passport, so don't go trying to contact them anymore."

I didn't react. But internally, my chest felt like a basketball had slammed it.

"That's how we located you and knew where you've been, although we can't prove anything else you've done illegally while traveling under a false passport. It was a happy coincidence to find you and Betty Snayer staying at the same place."

I turned my coffee mug round and round, making a scratching noise on the counter. It was no coincidence. Gus knew she'd come after me for something.

"The false passport alone could get you fifteen to twenty-five years."

I knew this. I was—had been—a lawyer. It was nothing more than a scare tactic. But hearing him say it made my mouth go dry.

"But if you agree to testify, I'll say you've been working for us as an informant."

I tried to keep an expression of boredom. I had no idea what to do.

Now he tried the silent treatment. One of us would cave.

But Tempest broke the impasse. She clawed at the door. Screw Ted. I let her in. For some reason, she wasn't afraid of Gus and walked past him to sit by my side, wet and dirty. I sighed. At least I could clean up *her* mess.

"I like that dog," Gus said.

I knew this wouldn't fly, but I tried anyway. "You don't need me to testify. You have the recordings."

"Do you want justice for your sister or not?"

I swallowed hard. What did he know about that?

"You've been on a mission, Ang. I get it. But you need to let us take the reins so that justice prevails."

I had so many rebuttals for that I couldn't choose. "What are you willing to give me, Gus? You put me in danger with Betty to get evidence and without my knowledge. I deserve full immunity. But the problem with me being a lawyer is I know you can't promise that."

Now he looked a little chagrined. Good. But he sighed and said, "I didn't want to tell you this, but if Sophie hadn't killed herself, Link would have killed her. On Betty's orders. Sophie knew too much."

Hearing this made Sophie's loss even worse. Hard as I tried not to cry, tears rolled down my cheeks. There had been no way out for my sister.

Before I could wipe away the tears, the door slammed open. Mike stepped in, a gun pointed at Gus. Tempest snapped but I grabbed her collar. She bared her teeth. Gus turned but not quick enough. Mike locked him in a choke-hold and put the pistol to his head. I didn't pull my gun for fear of shooting Gus. When Gus struggled, Mike said, "Don't, or I shoot the woman and the dog." Gus stopped. Mike forced him out the door, down the steps, and into the storm.

My heart pounded. I couldn't catch my breath. What was I going to do? I couldn't take on a hitman if an FBI agent couldn't. I closed the door before letting Tempest loose. I needed to get out of here. I yanked on shoes and raincoat. When I raced to the door and opened it, Betty stood there pointing a pistol at me, wet hair clinging to her head.

"Now maybe we can talk."

When Tempest lunged at her, the gun went off. Tempest yelped

I screamed. Something came down on my head.

64

W hen I came to, I was trussed up on the back seat of a car and not Betty's car. We navigated a rough road, passing Flame trees and *kukui*, no buildings, no highway sounds. My head throbbed and something sticky had trickled down my face and gone crusty. I could taste blood. I lost focus, closed my eyes, opened them again.

When I tried to move, I couldn't. I rolled to my side. Betty was driving. No Mike. No Gus.

"Hey, sunshine. How're you feeling?" Betty said this as if we were best friends on an outing.

"Did you kill my dog?"

"No, just grazed her. She'll be fine."

But why believe her? I managed to ask through cracked lips, "Where's Gus?"

"'Where's Gus?'" She mimiced. "My, aren't *you two* chummy. You mean Special Agent William Augustus Martin?"

I struggled to sit up and saw her in the rearview mirror, grinning, her eyes dark and glinty. We stopped along the dirt road near trees and brushy vegetation. Betty's car was parked there. Only the bumper was visible.

"Where are we?" I asked.

Betty killed the ignition, slipped her fingernail into a vial, and snorted god-knows-how-much coke. Then she licked her nail, pinched her nostrils, and lit a cigarette. "Sorry, hon. Can't share with you." She exhaled the smoke sideways as she jumped out of the SUV, headed toward her car, and disappeared, leaving a trail of cigarette smoke. The lettering on a sign nailed to a *kukui* tree was washed out. Brightly colored birds whistled and cawed.

I smelled the sea and the dank, rotting understory. Was this where I'd die? Had Mike killed Gus? Probably. I pulled at my ropes. I doubted if Betty knew how to tie anything, and I was right. My nails broke as I slowly worked on the rope around my wrists. One of the knots pried loose. Then I heard a gun go off. Once, twice. I had to bite back a scream. I pulled off the rest of the rope and undid my ankles. Sliding from the back seat, I opened the front passenger door and checked the console, then the glovebox where I found my loaded gun. I slipped it into the back of my jeans. I was sweating. My hand shook. My eyes blurred.

I wasn't sure which way to go. Or whether to hide. In those few seconds, Betty appeared. She pointed the gun and said, "I'll shoot if you move."

Sweat and blood dripped into my eyes. I swiped at them. Betty walked up and smiled. "You don't give up, do you?" The forced smile couldn't hide her jaws that scissored back and forth. Her eyes were glassy marbles. "OK, hon. I'm going to give you a second chance. Tell me where Gerard is and where he stashed the money. I know you know. I'm sure your sister told you before she died. No one leaves that kind of money behind."

"Wrong," I said. "I forfeited all the money from my husband's company. I wanted to be free of Link, my memory of seeing my sister hanging in her living room, the death of my husband."

"As the English say, bully for you, Ang. Let's walk."

She was so coked out she couldn't walk a straight line as she pushed me down a road that turned into a trail and out into a clearing. I didn't recognize any of it. We walked a long way. Three feral pigs scattered at our approach. The wind whipped at my face. I was tired, thirsty, and dizzy. A judge's gavel pounded inside my head. We moved toward the cliffs. Fuck. The ocean was hundreds of feet below. I stopped and pivoted. "Don't you think I'd tell you if I knew where the damn money was? I don't give a shit about it. I want to be left alone."

"Tell me about Gerard. What happened to him?"

"I killed him. That's what happened to him. I poisoned him."

She snorted like I was making this up. Then she stared at me and said, "What?"

"I thought he was the cause of my sister's suicide, so I changed my identity, went to Paris, found him, lured him in, and slipped him poison during New Year's celebration at the Eiffel Tower."

"You're not that clever."

"Why not? You believe I killed Link."

I could see the coke wearing off. She was jittery. She waved the gun around as she searched her pockets. Empty.

I lowered my voice as if talking to a client who was about to have a meltdown. "I was a criminal lawyer, Betty. I learned a lot from my clients."

The wind came up, and black clouds gathered on the

horizon. A seagull hovered above us, trying to fly against the wind. I was losing body heat.

"Move," she said, shoving the gun into my stomach.

I turned and reluctantly walked. The closer to the edge of the cliff, the harder the wind blew. The ocean roared below as it smashed against the rocks. High tide. It wouldn't matter that I was a dreadful swimmer. I'd be dead when I hit bottom. Either by a gunshot or—

"You insist there's nothing to tell me?" she said, her voice high and squeaky. "Last chance."

I turned toward her, hoping for a chance to use my gun. She pushed her hair aside without success.

"There's nothing to tell. Are you sure Link didn't hide it from *you*?"

That rattled her. The gun wavered, her eyes blinked rapidly. She pushed me closer toward the edge, her palm against my chest.

"What if I told you I know where it is?" I said. "What would you do? Neither of us has access to it. That died with Gerard and Sophie, or Link. So how could we find it?"

Shit. I'd just given her a reason to kill me right now. I had to think of something. Did I have time to reach into my pocket for the gun?

Betty chewed her lip. "I think you're lying," she said. She put the gun under my chin. Then I remembered—Betty's fear of spiders.

"Betty," I said, modulating my voice as I stared at her shoulder. "Don't move. A spider is crawling toward your neck."

She hesitated before looking over her shoulder in horror. I whipped an arm up and knocked the gun from her hand. Her fingernails found my face. I yanked her arm, whipped a leg under hers, and she fell. She looked up, squinted, and hissed. Then she lunged for my legs. I jumped aside.

She stumbled, tripped, tried to regain her footing but couldn't. Her arms flailed as she hung in the air for a second. I reached out, but she was already over the edge. And gone.

I couldn't look. I hugged myself and backed away from the cliff. I didn't hear a scream or cry. Even when the wind died. An image of Betty flashed through my head—her falling backward, smiling, waving to me as she floated like a leaf. I didn't want to see the reality.

I stepped back. When I was far enough away, I grabbed my stomach, nauseous, shaking. I had no idea where Mike was. He could be anywhere. I still was not safe.

65

I ran through the field, toward the road. When my legs turned to molasses, I slowed to a plod, not knowing if I should be going this way or away from the cars. I thought of Tempest and wondered if she were alive. I couldn't take it if she wasn't.

Up ahead, the SUV was in the distance, and someone approached. I pulled the gun from my pocket and pointed it at the figure. My hand shook. I couldn't see. I blinked. The person kept coming.

"Stop, or I'll shoot."

"It's OK, Ang." Muffled words. I couldn't make out the name.

I waved the gun. He knew my name. "Who are you?" I yelled.

"Don't shoot." More muffled words. The figure drew closer. "Ang? Say something." Closer. "Are you all right? Remember me?"

This time the words were clear. So was the accent.

Gerard.

I lowered the gun. Had I died? Was this a scene from "Lost?"

The face came into view. He wasn't dead. Not dead. When he stood in front of me, I stared. I touched his face, then his lips like I was trying to convince myself I wasn't dead.

I blurted out, "I'm sorry, so sorry." I searched his face for any sign that he knew I'd tried to poison him. I saw nothing. "What are you doing here?"

"Come. You need to sit. I'll explain everything."

I wanted Gerard to be alive. I did not want to come out of a coma and realize he *was* dead after all, and all of this had been a dream like a cheap-shot ending to a TV sitcom.

Gerard guided me over to Betty's rental. Two unmarked cars sat along the road behind it. A man at the second car talked on a cell. Gerard handed me bottled water. I drank.

"Is Gus dead?" I asked as if he knew who Gus was.

He nodded. "Yes, unfortunately."

I covered my face, exhausted and distraught.

"Is Betty dead?"

I dropped my arms to my side and whispered, "Yes. I—"

"Never mind that. You're hurt. You need medical attention."

"What about the guy who—"

"Found him next to Gus."

So those two shots. Betty fired them. Killed her hired man.

I looked up into those intelligent eyes. "Jesus," I said.

Gerard smiled. "No. Jesus is just fine."

I broke into laughter. My legs gave out, but he grabbed me and held me as my laughter turned to sobs.

66

Gerard wanted to take me to the hospital, but I said no. I demanded to go back to the Plantation to find Tempest. Besides, he needed to tell me everything. Everything.

I leaned my throbbing head back against the headrest.

"Don't close your eyes," he said. "You probably have a concussion."

For the first time, I realized I could have died, died a nasty death falling from the cliff as Betty had. Why did I feel nothing? Probably shock. Or maybe I was tired of all the fighting, running, and seeking justice for Sophie. At that moment, I wanted to scream—at both Sophie *and* Hank. Their bad choices had landed me here. God, I hated that phrase *bad choices*. As if choice was always rational.

I sat up and touched the bump on my head, my anger providing a jolt of energy. I peeked over at Gerard. Why and how was he alive? Where had he been all this time? How had he known where to find me? And Gus?

Or was it Betty who Gerard was after? And why? Who the hell *was* he?

He glanced in my direction and smiled. "At the Plantation, we'll clean the gash on your head and put some ice on it. You should see a doctor."

I was leery of him. No one was who they said they were. Not even me. But Gerard didn't mean me harm, or I'd be dead too. He hadn't taken my gun away either.

Even as weak as I felt, I noticed how stripped down Gerard was, just jeans and a plain t-shirt. I had to focus on something else.

The car. Just a black sedan, no siren, no additions, nothing. Probably identical to the other vehicle that had stayed at the scene. It had that new car smell, too. I wished I'd noticed the license plate. Something was fishy. My suspicions took over. Gerard was not innocent. Gerard might still be part of Betty's gang. Gerard may have been playing me all along. But for what? The money that Sophie'd left stashed in that Maryland account? It was a pittance. To take over Betty's syndicate? Possibly. With Gus and Link out of the way—

We pulled into the Plantation. Before the car came to a complete stop, I jumped out and raced to my cottage, leaving Gerard behind. All the dogs were there except Tempest. My heart sank. I snuffled back tears.

I yelled, "Tempest!"

I yelled a few more times before she came out from under the porch. I squatted, laughing and crying, as she pressed her head against my chest. She was muddy. So was the wound to her shank, but it was only a flesh wound and the dried mud had stopped the bleeding.

From behind, Gerard said, "Looks like you both need a doctor."

On the porch, Tempest curled up on her blanket. I wiped my bloody face on my shirt and went inside. Gerard followed. I pulled the gun from the back of my jeans and pointed it at him. I wondered if the audio in the gun was still recording and where the recording was going.

"Sit," I said to Gerard. "Now explain. Every detail."

He circled one of the living room chairs and sat like a class act. I perched on the edge of my chair by the window.

"Angeline, you have nothing to be afraid of."

"I've been told that lie too many times."

He sighed. "Can I start at the beginning?"

"First, I want to know if you loved Sophie."

He rubbed his face and swallowed hard. There was pain there. "Yes," he said. "I did. That was something I couldn't foresee. It changed everything."

I wiped my nose on my sleeve, a deep sadness sinking into my chest, but I kept the gun trained on him. "OK. What happened?"

67

For the next half hour, Gerard talked about what he'd known and had done. He'd worked for the French government agency that was similar to the FBI. The economic agency was his cover. Like Gus, he'd tried to bust Betty and Link.

"Link looked to expand by attending international economic fairs. I started attending them too. That's how I met him," he said. "Are you sure you're OK?"

"Go on," I prompted, not wanting to admit that I felt a little sick.

He gave me a dubious look, but continued. "Link tried to use a French dating site for married people, but he gave that up because he didn't speak French. When he met me, he saw a gold mine. He even said, 'A handsome Frenchman. I bet you're a magnet for the ladies.'" Gerard rolled his eyes. "My cover in the economic development agency and its contacts with major businesses made it impossible for him to resist. He saw how lucrative that would be."

Gerard paused. He seemed preoccupied, not with the

story, but something else. My nausea increased, but I had to hear this.

"I saw him a few times at these fairs, and we went out in the evenings. Whatever he did, I went along, like picking up women and snorting cocaine. One night when we were drunk and high, I pretended to be tired of working for a government agency that was all about money-money-money. I told him people like me made rich people richer while I couldn't afford to buy a house in Paris. That drew him out. He confided in me. He told me about his 'outlaw' group—yes, he used that word. They robbed the rich and gave to the poor. It was all I could do not to laugh. Such *merde*. He explained he and his wife didn't need the money. They were wealthy. He even introduced me to Betty."

Through my dizziness, I managed to ask, "So what happened with my sister?"

He pressed his fingers to his eyes. "I met Sophie at a convention in L.A. and, as you Americans say, fell hard. We secretly rendezvoused although I knew I was putting her in jeopardy." He sighed heavily this time. "I stayed with her for a weekend in Eugene. She told you she was out of town. We talked about the future. She wasn't supposed to talk about our relationship, not even to you. I made up a story that I was in the middle of a very contentious divorce with a custody battle, so having an affair could make it difficult for me."

"She showed me a photo of you and her," I said. "I wasn't happy about it, but she was truly gaga over you and what could I say? She never listened to reason. I blamed you for her suicide. Then I discovered she was screwing my husband."

"She did that to protect you. Link told her if she didn't

find a way to steal from your husband's company, you'd have an 'accident.' You do know that Link was capable of murder?"

I lowered the gun. "Then what happened?"

"Link must have sensed something. I think that's why he drugged us and videoed the *ménage à trois* when we were at the Miami convention."

"Why?"

"He used that 'fun' night to turn her against me. Told her I set her up and only pretended to love her. Afterward, he said I could never see or communicate with Sophie. He would kill her if I did." He picked dog hair from the chair, looked at it then brushed it from his hand. "I couldn't tell her the truth, not until Betty and Link were behind bars. I had to protect her."

Why hadn't he died from the poison? Maybe I shouldn't ask. But I had to know. "What about Paris? What about us?"

He lit a cigarette without asking and blew smoke to the ceiling. "When you came to Paris, I knew who you were. Sophie showed me photos of you. Your disguise only worked with people who didn't know you. I had you followed. I thought perhaps you used a disguise for safety. Link was still a threat. I waited for you to give me a message from Sophie, but I didn't understand why you didn't reveal who you were right away. So I had to find out your intention." He squinted. "With the blonde wig and makeup, you looked so much like her." He flicked ash into his palm. "I waited and waited, but no message."

"There was no message."

He choked on a drag from his cigarette then cleared his throat. Stuttering at first he said, "Remem ... remember when we were at the Opera House? I tried to draw you out. I

knew how much she loved *The Phantom of the Opera.* I
missed her, and you were right there, and I kissed you.
Désolé."

So he had been head over heels for my sister. I couldn't
hold the gun anymore, so I laid it on the side table.

He leaned forward and examined his hands. "Then as
you and I toured Château de Vaux le Vicomte, you said—
and I remember your words—'My sister died not long ago. I
miss her.'"

"Oh, God, I did?"

"I didn't know Sophie was dead. I pulled you to me, not
only to comfort you, but also to hide my reaction. I'm not
sure what happened after that. All I could think of was that
Link had killed her, and I would get even."

I struggled to keep my balance on the arm of the chair,
but Gerard didn't notice. He was thinking of Sophie.

He suddenly stood and ran fingers through his hair.
"Later, I looked for Sophie's obituary and discovered. ..."

His words trailed off. Outside a myna bird made its
raucous noise and fueled my headache. Gerard struggled to
continue.

"When New Year's happened, I understood. You wanted
revenge. You thought I was to blame. I saw you fiddle with
my glass. I dumped the champagne without you seeing,
pretended to be poisoned, gagged, coughed, gurgled and
spit up. You're an amateur in my world, Angeline. You didn't
check my pulse or breath." He stood over me. "I'm sorry you
lost your sister. She loved you very much. She called you her
'warrior sister.'"

I didn't have the heart to tell him she'd been pregnant
when she died. My eyesight blurred. I couldn't see. I slid off
the arm of the chair and into the seat. I mumbled, "Sophie
thought you were in with Link. She died not knowing how

much you loved her." I leaned forward and held my head in my hands. I thought of my sister and how life had cheated her when real love had come along. Gerard said something, but I didn't understand. I couldn't focus. The room spun. I fell off the chair, and everything went dark.

68

The hospital lights hurt my eyes. My head no longer pounded but the bump was still there. My mouth was so dry I could hardly swallow. Next to the bed, a hospital water jug and straw. I drank.

A nurse stepped up to the bed. She checked the monitors and intravenous. "Are you hungry? Can I order a meal tray for you?"

"Yes," I croaked. "How did I get here?"

"Someone dropped you off at ER."

So he hadn't stayed.

"Could you turn down the lights, please?"

She did.

A friendly face peeked around the door. "Hi, River."

It was Iolana from the library.

She held a bouquet of Birds-of-paradise.

The next morning before I headed home, I was ordered to take it easy for the next few days and no driving for forty-eight hours. The doctor had found no bleeding or fractured skull. He said it was a "standard" concussion, whatever the hell that was.

I took a taxi back to the Plantation. The driver helped me to my cottage. He smiled and insisted on carrying my flowers. All the dogs were there. Tempest limped a little.

In my fridge, someone had left a bento box, seaweed salad, and fresh pineapple juice. Who? A note from Iolana. "The people from the market wish you a speedy recovery. Aloha."

For the next few days, I listened to local radio news and scanned the paper for the murders. Nothing. I sat by the pool in one of the white Adirondack chairs, napped, and read. On the third day, the news finally reported that tourists had found three bodies. The police called it accidental, three *haoles* who hadn't listened to the warnings about the island dangers. How they'd come up with this was beyond me.

Unfortunately, feral pigs got to them first. It would take weeks to identify them. A drone sited the third body at the bottom of the cliff, a female, battered almost beyond recognition.

So Gerard and his compatriots had done nothing about it. Maybe he was never supposed to be there in the first place. Or perhaps it was enough for him to report to Paris. I was tired of trying to figure out every clandestine move or shadow play.

A week passed. I waited for someone to knock on my door, to place me at the scene, to connect me somehow with Gus or Betty, but nothing happened. Always in the back of my mind, I worried that Gus had left info about me, maybe that recording. I doubted it. I trusted Gus hadn't turned me in. Nothing more was reported about the three bodies. Someone shut that down.

Island chatter also died. People returned to talking about their favorite television show, a Korean drama, "Rebel:

Thief Who Stole the People." Iolana talked about it like she knew the characters personally. The story was of Hong Gil Dong, often said to be the Robin Hood of Korea. The irony wasn't lost on me. I was tempted to tell her about an American couple, the so-called Robin Hood form they'd taken, how warped that was. Of course I didn't. I did tell her I was bored and needed to do something that mattered. I needed distraction. Doing something that mattered would be a change.

I tried contacting Snoop again, but she never called back. I hoped she was all right. I was restless. Couldn't stop thinking about Gerard, who he really was, how unfair and unjust life was.

I carried a cocktail and a book to the beach. I ran fingers through my growing hair. Tempest chased one of the moas, a wild chicken, but she couldn't catch it because of her lame leg. I was sure she had hunted and ate moas after being abandoned. Kept her alive. We did whatever was necessary.

"Aloha! Are you River?"

I stood and lowered my sunglasses. A tall, broad-shouldered man approached. He had to be of Samoan descent. I couldn't tell how old he was. His smile was infectious. I smiled back.

"Yes. And you?"

"Iolana told me you might be interested in helping us."

He was a member of an island group fighting corporations that had taken over the island, brought GMO crops here, and sprayed tons of toxic pesticides a year. What once had been fields of sugar cane and pineapple were now predominantly corn seed crops.

His name was Aisake. He lowered onto the sand near my chair. I asked him what his name meant. He grinned, drew in the sand, and said, "He who laughs." Then he laughed. He was delightful.

He told me about the group, divulged that sometimes the group walked a thin line between legal and illegal. "But when up against giants," he said, "a slingshot sometimes is necessary."

"Sounds like my kind of battle."

I told him I had a legal background, but not that I had been a lawyer. He volunteered to pick me up tomorrow and take me around the island to show me what they were fighting.

After he left, I walked back to the cottage. This type of battle could be exciting, stimulating. Tomorrow I had planned to visit some rentals. I needed to move. I'd put it off for too long. But I'd do that the following day. Besides, Aisake might know about better places to rent.

The scent of plumeria wafted past. The sun reflected off the living room windows, lighting them to a burnt gold. I mixed another drink and remembered the Portland Hotel Vintage and the barman who had concocted my cocktail for the city's contest. Then I remembered the night with Gus, and I cried.

I lit a candle for Gus. I had no idea what I believe happened after death, but over the candle I said, "Gus, you were one of the good guys. You may not have been the greatest lover—or me either for that fact—but the circumstances weren't the best, were they?" I chuckled, then drew in a breath and let go. "Thank you for saving my life." I paused, picturing him when we first met, him wearing that absurd '60s outfit. I wondered what would happen to his Thunderbird. I wondered if he'd had a family. I wondered where he lived and what he'd done as a hobby or sport. At least Gus had been one of the most real people I'd met in all this mess. "OK, big guy. So long for now."

On the porch, I scratched Tempest under the chin. Memories rewound, back to Paris. The Catacombs, the Chateau, the seafood dinner with Gerard. I loved Paris, even as I plotted to kill Gerard. What a juxtaposition. But why think of Paris and Gerard now? Let the past stay the past. I pushed my mind forward and reviewed what Aisake and I talked about, excited to picture a future instead of running from the past. That night I slept better than I had in years.

The next morning I jumped out of bed before sunrise. I ate my granola on the top step, enjoying the light of day as it brought everything into detail. A Laughing Thrush sang in a nearby iron tree. I wondered what to wear today. It felt good to have my hair longer and tickle my neck. I laughed for no reason. I threw a stick for the dogs.

After my shower and change of clothes, someone knocked at the door. I checked my phone. Maybe Aisake was early. I opened the door. A stranger stood there. I didn't open the screen.

"River Atwood?"

I didn't answer. The dogs were gone. I looked for any clue as to who he was.

"Are you River Atwood?" He looked down at something in his hands.

I wondered if he was serving me papers.

"I have a package for you."

There was no logo on his shirt. "Are you UPS or FedEx?"

"Private delivery."

"Who's it from?"

"I don't know."

"What do you mean 'I don't know?' You have to know."

Now I wished I had a lock on my screen, not that it would do any good.

"No, ma'am. I'm just the courier."

No way was I going to accept that package.

"Send it back," I said just before closing the door and locking it.

My hands shook, and I sat at the counter, wondering what the hell had been in that brown envelope.

Aisake arrived. I was so relieved to see him. Over the next few hours, we toured the island's agricultural areas. I made notes. Aisake pointed out a few rental places. He said I could use his name as a reference. I added these to my notebook too.

On our way to lunch, we passed a guy standing at an intersection. The guy was dressed as the Grim Reaper—black cape, flaming red death mask—and held a sign in dripping red lettering that read, "Monsanto Sucks!"

Aisake said he was a regular and haunted different roadways at busy times. For some reason, the Grim Reaper reminded me of the homeless Santa I'd seen in Paris. I shuddered.

We ate lunch at a local place where everyone knew Aisake, and I looked through a file he gave me. He openly answered my questions and asked if I'd like to attend one of their meetings.

I didn't know if I would. I didn't know what I was doing. I was afraid that if I became involved, someone would find out my legal identity and that could lead to. ... For a moment, my mind drifted like an unmoored boat. He continued to eat.

Finally, I said, "I'm not sure."

We cut the afternoon short as a storm built and headed

toward the island. I realized I hadn't thought about the package all afternoon.

But when he dropped me off at the cottage, I found the package wedged between the screen and front door. I held it out for Tempest to sniff. She didn't react. Inside, I sat in my chair by the window with the damn thing in my lap. I smelled it—a hint of exhaust fumes, brown paper, and male sweat, not island scents. The sun struggled with a black horizon. Blood-red streaks were reflected below in the dark ocean. I turned on the table lamp. I opened the envelope.

A passport fell out, along with a birth certificate, a U.S. driver's license, and a note. I gasped. It was my photo and pseudonym on the passport and license. River Atwood. I'd never seen this photo before. The documents looked legit. I opened the handwritten note.

River,
    In hopes that you'll join me in Paris. Please don't wait long.
    Gerard

There was a phone number at the bottom. I shoved everything back into the envelope.

69

I stood on the porch as the storm hit. The dogs had already taken shelter from the slap of rain and wind, the whipping trees, the wild ocean. I was soaked. I struggled to stand. My shirt ballooned in the wind. My bare feet tried to keep their grip. I backed toward the door and had to wrestle with both the screen and the inside door to open and close them.

Inside, I headed to the bathroom. Paris. Gerard. Could this be the chance to recreate my visit, to start over? I shivered, stripped, dried off, wrapped in a blanket, and dumped the envelope's contents on my kitchen counter. Outside the storm pummeled the porch. Trees bent. The wind whistled and howled around the cottage.

As I looked at the passport and my photo, I didn't recognize the woman there. How had he come by this photo? My spiky colored hair was a thing of the past. I was sick of all this deviousness.

I doubted if he'd reported my involvement with Betty and Link. Why I didn't know. Maybe he'd felt it unnecessary. Maybe he figured I'd been through enough. But what if he hadn't reported me because he'd had other plans for me, personal ones.

Who was I kidding? Gerard was not interested in me. I'd been a substitute for Sophie. I wouldn't be starting over. I'd be going backward. I'd love to change the past, but I couldn't. I needed a fresh start.

I tore strips of newspaper, piled them in the sink, and dumped Gerard's note and the envelope's contents on top.

But when I lit a match, I couldn't do it. Something told me not to. What if I needed these documents in the future to prove something legally? What did I honestly know about Gerard? What if he was trying to get me back to Paris to arrest me for attempting to kill him? He showed up on the island then disappeared. Why? My trust had been compromised, not in the law, not about justice, but in humans. I shoved everything into a bag and stuffed it into a suitcase. Some day, if I ever had to escape, I'd have my documentation.

After the storm passed, I walked the wet beach with Tempest. Maybe I could fight for something better. As Hank used to say after he left corporate America to strike out on his own, he wanted to fight the good fight. I could try to do something worthwhile here on the island, something that would require more than a slingshot at these corporate bastards.

If I had to go down, I wanted to go down in a fight that was worth fighting.

When I returned to the cottage, the phone rang. I answered, expecting Iolana or Aisake, and said, "Hi, I've been—"

"Allo, Angeline. Can you talk?" It was Gerard.

Could I? Would I? I sat and bit a nail. My heart pounded at the sound of his voice. But was it a good pounding? No. I jumped up and kicked the cupboard. He'd given me his number so I could call him. Now he was calling me? This was *my* choice. No one was moving me around like a chess piece ever again. I was done.

I heard him breathing, waiting. I hung up.

AFTERWORD

Will Angeline return in a second novel? Who knows?

You can! Sign up at www.valeriejbrooks.com for your freebie and find out what's next. Ang or someone else?

The best words an author can hear? "I loved this novel!" and "I didn't want it to end."

If you feel the same way, please leave a message on the contact page at www.valeriejbrooks.com and write a review on Goodreads and any of the bookseller sites.

Readers and fans keep the energy and words flowing. It's the lifeblood of an author to be read, enjoyed, and appreciated.

Thank you for reading *Revenge in 3 Parts*.

ACKNOWLEDGMENTS

Love, gratitude, and thanks go to:

Best pal and co-conspirator, Jan Eliot, creator of the internationally syndicated cartoon strip "Stone Soup."

My stellar LitChix writing group: Chris Scofield, author of *The Shark Curtain*, and Patsy Hand, author of *Lost Dogs of Rome*.

For support in so many ways: Tom Titus, Jessica Maxwell, Randy Sue Coburn, Lois Jean Bousquet, Barbara Sullivan, Susan Glassow, Kirsten Steen, Grace Elting Castle, Mike Sobol, Evelyn Hess, Cynthia Pappas, Olivia Klassen, Terry Brix, Mary Jo Comins, Karla Droste, Linda Leslie, Marlene Howard, Samantha Ducloux Waltz, Jill Sager, Quinton Hallett, JoJo Jensen, Kent Brooks, Debby Brooks, Tracy Miller, Anne Delon, Patrick Salisbury, Rhiannon Daniel, and Valerie Ihsan.

Kirsten Steen and Ed Gressett. You know why.

Jason Holden. You also know why.

Laura White, steadfast supporter and advocate for

authors. Plus, the University of Oregon Duckstore bookstore staff.

Will Branscomb my expert on all things computer and internet security.

Kirsten Steen & Judith Watt for graciously letting me use their photos.

Howard Robertson & Margaret Robertson for the opportunity to read at the Lane Community Readers Series.

Scott Landfield and Tsunami Books for keeping the faith and continuing to give writers and authors a home base.

Wendy Kendall & Julie Cooper for interviewing me on the podcast series "Kendall and Cooper Talk Mysteries."

Cindy Casey & the fabulous crew at Vero Café; Barnes & Noble; Tap & Growler.

Oregon Writers Colony for providing a second home and writing retreat at Colonyhouse in Rockaway Beach, Oregon; Wordcrafters; Willamette Writers; Pacific Northwest Writers Association; and Sisters in Crime.

Elizabeth George Foundation for a grant that led me to writing noir.

The residencies that gave me time and immersion to explore my writing: Hedgebrook for Women, Playa, Villa Montalvo for the Arts, Soapstone, and Vermont Studio Center.

My family. You lift me up and carry me along, always.

My pooch, Stevie Nicks, who took over one of my writing desks but has been a lousy editor.

My one and only, my heart and soul mate, Dan Connors, the best traveling companion and scout ever.

ABOUT THE AUTHOR

Award-winning author VALERIE J BROOKS has published in *Scent of Cedars: Thirty-two Promising Writers from the Pacific Northwest* and *France, a Love Story: Women Write About the French Experience.*

She received an Elizabeth George Foundation grant and the Monticello Award for Creative Writing. As a literary activist, she served as Associate Fiction Editor at *Northwest Review* for four years, was a Board of Directors member of Oregon Writers Colony and Eugene Ballet, was an advisor for Artists in Schools program, and co-founded Willamette Writers Speakers Series.

Valerie enjoys life in Oregon with a nearby large family and lives on the McKenzie River with her husband Daniel Connors and their spirited Havanese pooch Stevie Nicks.

PLEASE SIGN UP ON VALERIE'S WEBSITE TO RECEIVE HER NEWSLETTER PLUS JOIN HER ON FACEBOOK for giveaways, noir news, interesting noir fiction & film facts, and freebies.

FOLLOW VALERIE AT
    www.valeriejbrooks.com
    facebook.com/noirtravelstories
    pinterest.com/valinparis/
    twitter.com/ValinParis
    instagram.com/ValinParis/